Christie Malry's Own Double-Entry

Christie Malry's Own Double-Entry

B. S. Johnson

A RICHARD SEAVER BOOK

The Viking Press
New York

A Richard Seaver Book / The Viking Press

Published in 1973 by The Viking Press, Inc.
625 Madison Avenue, New York, N.Y. 10022

SBN 670-22013-2

Library of Congress catalog card number: 73-4172
Printed in U.S.A.

Contents

CHAPTER I

The Industrious Pilgrim: an Exposition without which You might have felt Unhappy

Christie Malry was a simple person.

It did not take him long to realise that he had not been born into money; that he would therefore have to acquire it as best he could; that there were unpleasant (and to him unacceptable) penalties for acquiring it by those methods considered to be criminal by society; that there were other methods not (somewhat arbitrarily) considered criminal by society; and that the course most likely to benefit him would be to place himself next to the money, or at least next to those who were making it. He therefore decided that he should become a bank employee.

I did tell you Christie was a simple person.

At the interview formally granted to all new employees by one of the bank's General Managers at Head Office, Christie's minimal qualifications were laid bare, his appearance scrutinised, and his nervousness remarked on. Then he was asked why he wished to join the bank. Christie was lost, could not think of his answer. One was shortly supplied for him: most young men joined the bank for the security, for the very liberal pension which amounted to two-thirds of whatever salary the employee was receiving at retiring age. And this retiring age itself was as an act of generosity sixty, and not sixty-five!

Not only was Christie simple, he was young, too, a few

weeks past his seventeenth birthday at the time of this interview.

Christie was silent even at the information that he had only forty-three and not forty-eight years to wait before he was free. The whole impetus of the interview was towards his providing a standard set of correct answers: or of losing points for wrong answers. Did Christie have to play? The General Manager made him very much aware of his power. What Christie thought, however (and how privileged we are to be able to know it) was that he would consider himself to be a failure if he had to depend on a bank pension at sixty; and that it would show a remarkable lack of spirit even to be thinking, at the age of seventeen, of pensions and retirement. The truth, that he was interested in placing himself next to some money, seemed not to be required in the context. The offices of a General Manager of one of the few national banks is not the place to exeleutherostomise.

From this you might think that Christie was mad for money as some are mad for sex: but that is not so. Christie, like almost all of us, had to think of earning a living first; the economics dictate to an extent sometimes not fully realised the real (as distinct from the imaginary) possibilities open to one to move in other directions. But be assured that sex was one of the things for which Christie wanted money; sex was always, particularly at this age, one of the things he thought about most, had very often in mind.

Christie was accepted into the service of the bank despite his inadequacy at providing the correct answers; his failure to give any answers at all did not count against him as much as a succession of wrong answers. And, for reasons Christie was just about to experience for himself, the bank had difficulty in holding on to recruits of his age and therefore deliberately took on far more than it knew would stay the long course to early retirement and two-thirds of an honest penny.

So Christie started at the Hammersmith branch (conveniently near his home) of this nationally-known concern one Monday morning in October. From the comparative shelter of his school (of which I shall probably not tell you much) it was a painful transposition. Christie had expected to have to work hard, and to find the work both uncongenial and menial, at first. What he did not expect was the atmosphere in which he was expected to work, and which was created by his fellow-employees or colleagues as they were in the habit of calling one another. This atmosphere was acrid with frustration, boredom and jealousy, black with acrimony, pettiness and bureaucracy. It was partly a result of the obsolescence of the premises in which the bank had set out to carry on business: for despite the modernity of computer-based accounts and to every colleague his own personal adding machine, the original investment in mahogany, marble and brass had been so great as to make it impossible to sweep it away and think about banking all over again.

In this atmosphere Christie quickly became bitter and unhappy himself. Nor did he feel himself to be nearer, in any sense that mattered, money. His job consisted of listing the amounts of cheques on an adding machine and at the end of the day agreeing his total with that of the cashiers. Two days out of three it did not agree; and on these days he had to go through the cheques again, calling the amounts to a girl who checked them on the list until they found the error. Sometimes they could shorten the process by looking for an exact amount that had been missed or included twice. But this was rare. Usually it would be a variation in the decimal point one way or the other which would throw the whole thing out. Very rarely indeed it would be the cashier who had made an error and not Christie.

The girl's name was Margaret. She made the tea: Christie was not as lowly as that. On the other hand, he was not allowed to open the post in the morning; while he was allowed to seal it at night. Opening and sealing are not the same: Christie was quite clear as to his preference, but there was no chance of his being allowed to exercise it.

The Manager of the branch Christie most infrequently saw; he remained in his office and summoned underlings. Christie did not rank high enough to be an underling, in this sense. The Chief Accountant and the Assistant Accountant hardly noticed Christie either, except to lambaste him icily on those occasions when totals did not agree or when he (as often happened) committed some other banking solecism.

The clerks and cashiers formed a closed, median group: they were mature men and women, tiny.

The only colleague apart from Margaret who spoke to Christie at times other than when he had made a mistake was Joan. Joan was nineteen, plain, androgynous and Christie's immediate superior. She it was who showed him how to operate his (it had been her) adding machine, she who showed him where he could have coffee in the mornings and tea in the afternoons, she with whom as time went on (and it did, in this case, go on for a short while) he could share a small joke at the expense of a cashier who had (say) ten pounds more than he should have done at the end of the working day.

Christie was invited to join the Staff Association. He understood that there was a real trade union in banking, but that the banks also ran their own and called them Staff Associations.

Even at this politically unaware stage of his life Christie could see through that one. The invitation was given an added irony by the fact that it was made by the man most likely to cause grievance for which Christie might approach a Staff Association to seek redress: the Chief Accountant.

Nevertheless, Christie joined. Again, the invitation posed a question which expected only a correct answer; and silence was not this time acceptable. So a small sum was deducted each week from Christie's wages and placed to the credit of the Staff Association account. Christie's wages themselves were minimal: it was explained to him that this was to compensate for the utter security of his job. Other companies and institutions were fly-by-night, compared. A man might work for them for forty years and then find himself on the street, unemployed. What a prospect!

Christie still found it hard to take, hard to live. He looked forward to his eighteenth birthday when a small rise was promised, if not due. When it came, he found it was cancelled out with a book-keeping preciseness and copperplate neatness by an increase, now he counted as adult, in the amount of his contributions to national health insurance and the Staff Association.

At Xmas there was a bonus, which in Christie's case amounted to enough for him to buy his mother a bottle of sherry. Christie was there for Xmas, it so happened, he had not yet acquired sufficient courage to give and serve notice: this was to come, in the spring.

As for the money, Christie was soon certain that he was not appreciably nearer to it. Indeed, he very soon experienced that curious distancing effect felt by honest persons in a similar situation: the money he saw in piles and sacks was virtually a different thing from those notes and coins that he had in his own pockets. And those paper transactions with which he partially dealt did not make much real sense either: he would think hard about why J. Seminole Ltd had paid £53.48 to the firm of solicitors who were tenants of the chambers above the bank, and of course within the bank it was not possible for him to find out. It made, he thought, a mockery of the oath of secrecy as to matters concerning clients' business he had been required to sign on joining the bank. No doubt the Manager knew secrets, no doubt the Chief Accountant was privy to some of them as well; but none were allowed to filter down as far as Christie. The nearest he came to a secret was in over-hearing the cashiers and clerks discussing some share value which had oscillated oddly; and by the time bank clerks were talking about such a thing loudly enough for anyone to overhear, it was no longer a secret anyway.

So Christie thought again. And in his direct way he merely modified his approach: he decided the way to move nearer to money was to become an accountant, in order to see where the money came from, how it was manipulated, and where it went.

A simple man, as I have too often said.

Christie saw his move in two parts. The first was to pass up the sheltering lifelong security offered by the bank and to seek his fortune in one of those rash new companies which had been established less than a couple of centuries. The other was to embark on a course of study leading to examinations which, if passed, would give him a professional qualification as an accountant.

In the spring Christie accordingly served out his month's notice at the bank, well survived the open contempt of the colleagues, who clearly thought he was a waster (or something equally as oldfashioned as the bank's façade) and particularly the dismay of Joan, who never spoke to him once during the month. And there was no coin collection made for Christie, no farewell cakes with the last afternoon tea, no warm handshakes or promises to meet in the near future over lunch or a drink.

But Christie had learnt a lot at the bank. It was hardly apparent to him at the time; it would be of great value later on.

Christie's new job was also in Hammersmith and not far from the bank, as it happened. Tapper's had been manufacturing sweets and cakes for a mere eighty-three years, and they were short of an invoice clerk after all that time. Christie was the only respondent to their advertisement: he thought it might be just what he needed.

In the evenings Christie would work at the correspondence course in Accountancy for which he had enrolled. Almost at once he was made aware of the system of Double-Entry which was (though some time later) to give him his Great Idea and influence the course of his life so radically.

Although evidence of some form of recording accounts is found in many older civilisations, the first man known to have codified the method called Double-Entry Book-keeping was Fra Luca Bartolomeo Pacioli, a Tuscan monk and a contemporary of Leonardo da Vinci. Pacioli included his account of accounts in a much larger mathematical work, *Suma de Arithmetica, Geometria Proportioni et Proportionalità*, which was printed in Venice in 1494 and therefore qualifies as incunabula. It is now most easily available in a translation published by the Institute of Book-keepers and Related Data Processing Ltd, to whom I am myself a debtor for permission to quote. The exposition of this novel would not be complete without an extract from this prime source:

TO THE respectful subjects of the Duke of Urbino, so that they may have all the rules of Mercantile order they may need, I have prepared another particular treatise, very necessary to compile. The present treatise will serve all their needs with regard to accounts and recording, and for this reason only do I insert it. I therefore intend to give sufficient rules to enable them to keep all their accounts and books in an orderly manner. As is known, three things are necessary to one who wishes diligently to carry on business. Of these the most important is cash, or any other substantial power, without which the carrying on of business is very difficult.

It has happened that many, entering business with nothing but good faith, have yet carried on big business; and through their credit, faithfully served, they have attained to greater wealth. In our conversations with persons throughout Italy, we have come across many of these; and in the great republics the word of a good merchant is considered sufficient, and oaths are taken on it saying: 'it is the word of a real merchant.' This cannot be admiration, as catholically everybody is saved by faith, without which it is impossible to please God.

The second thing looked for in business is to be a good accountant and sharp book-keeper and to arrive at this, as we have seen above, we have regular rules and canons necessary to each operation, so that any diligent reader can understand all by himself. If one does not understand this well, the following would serve him in vain.

The third and last thing necessary is that all one's affairs be arranged in good order so that one may get, without loss of time, all particulars as to the Debit and also the Credit of all of them, as business does not deal with anything else. This is very useful, because it would be impossible to conduct business without due order of recording; for without rest, merchants would always be in great mental trouble. Therefore I have arranged this treatise wherein I give the method of recording all kinds of entries, proceeding chapter by chapter; and as I cannot put down all that ought to be written on the subject, nevertheless an industrious pilgrim will be able to apply it to any other required case.

CHAPTER II

Here is Christie's Great Idea!

Christie Malry, after a long day largely spent feeding pieces of paper into various machines, is making his way home from Tapper's office and contemplating the sublime symmetry of Double-Entry the while.

For the following passage it seems to me necessary to attempt transcursion into Christie's mind; an illusion of transcursion, that is, of course, since you know only too well in whose mind it all really takes place.

Who made me walk this way?   Who decided I should not be walking seven feet farther that side, or three points west of nor-nor-east, to use the marine abbreviation?   Anyone?   No one?   Someone must have decided. It was a conscious decision, as well. That is, they said (he said, she said), I will build here.   But I think whoever it was did not also add, So Christie Malry shall not walk here, but shall walk there. If he chooses. Ah! And there I have him/her/them! If I choose so. But my choice is limited by them, collectively, to a certain extent.

I shall list my choices. I may choose to walk for some forty feet along this particular stretch of pavement at a width of approximately eight feet. On one side my freedom is limited by my desire not to be hit by traffic. On the other by whoever built this no doubt speculative office

23

block.   *The first limitation I accept, forced on me reasonably enough by society. The other I do not accept.*

    Who can I blame? The person who took this decision which clearly does me no good is probably no longer alive. But his successors, heirs, executors, administrators, personal representatives and assigns certainly are, or they would not be here, in business. They are not averse to taking responsibility for all the money they/he/she left them, so they may conveniently take responsibility for standing this building in my way, too, limiting my freedom of movement, dictating to me where I may or may not walk in this street.

    I could express it in Double-Entry terms, Debit receiver, Credit giver, the Second Golden Rule, Debit Christie Malry for the offence received, Credit Office Block for the offence given.   *How settle that account?*

    I am entitled to exact payment, of course. Every Debit must have its Credit, the First Golden Rule.   *But payment in what form?*

Christie turned and walked back, against the flow of the crowd, past the office block again. He stopped and took a coin from his pocket and, keeping close to the wall whilst holding the coin down at arms' length, he scratched an unsightly line about a yard long into the blackened portland stone facing of the office block.

    Debit them, Credit me!   *Account settled!*

Christie walked on as though nothing had happened, no one had noticed.   No one had!

But Christie almost shouted aloud at his discovery:

    It's a Great Idea! Eureka! My very own Double-Entry!

CHAPTER III

Ave Atque Vale to Christie's Mother

Christie lived with his mother at this point, near Hammersmith Bridge, in the stump of Mall Road left after the flyover and associated highway improvements.

When he arrived home on this day (time now being more or less continuous) his mother rose and welcomed him. Then she delivered herself of a statement, thus:

'My son: I have for the purposes of this novel been your mother for the past eighteen years and five months to the day if I assume your conception to have taken place after midnight. Now that you have had your Great Idea and are set upon your life's work there is nothing further for me to do.'

Christie's mother paused. Then continued.

'I do not complain. I have every reason to be satisfied with what I have done. I have cared for you without cosseting, cooked sensibly for you without running risks from whatever disease was fashionably connected with food at each of several times. Those parts of my body under taboos ruling over the last quarter of a century have not been exposed to you since at latest the age of three. I have, husbandless, brought you up not to miss a father, without damaging what they would call your normality. I flatter myself that you are yourself, that you are both more and less than what I have made you, if that means anything. Nor have I let your character be moulded by such other men as I have allowed (for I am not a wooden block) to cross my path and enter in at the shrine of my womanhood. The rather fanciful conceit is used to spare your blushes, Christie, for sons in general have to be over thirty before they can talk without embarrassment to their mothers about sexual matters. Or anything else, I have sometimes (in moments of cynicism) thought.'

Again the charming old lady paused, reflected, and went on:

'I even allowed you to keep a pet, a cat, in order to encourage some kind of loving in you, despite the fact that Austin inevitably meant more work for me in skinning and braising the mice and other small creatures he regularly brought in. Fortunately for you, Austin passed over four months before the occasion of this statement I am at present making, so you are thus spared, Christie, the expense of having him put to sleep at the veterinary surgery. But how I laughed when you first lisped, "I do love pussy!" '

And the old lady permitted a sudden smile to illuminate her smooth, lined face. Christie smiled, too, as his mother resumed:

'We have not always lived here. It is important for them to bear that in mind, Christie, if they are to understand. Not that I necessarily want them to understand, but it is clearly desirable that you should have the choice of allowing them to understand if you so wish. No, we have lived elsewhere. We lived when you were between the ages of six and nine on the outskirts of a small town in a house with a railway line at the bottom of the garden. There were only two trains a day, and indeed they were really the same one: to the jam factory, there and back on the single track. But I break into rhyme . . .'

The old lady showed signs of annoyance, and playfully slapped the back of one hand with the other before going on:

'You soon learnt to place pennies on the track and observe how the loaded trains would flatten them more than the returning ones. Oh, we had pennies and to spare, then! And a hole in the fence, too, on to railway property. What days they were! In no time at all you were experimenting with pieces of broken milkbottle on the rail to perfect a very cheap manufacturing process for powdered glass. How proud I was of you when you showed such remarkable precocity in using pieces of poison and other coloured glass bottles to produce powders of such delicate and attractive hues!'

The old lady seemed lost in thought for a moment, the rich memories bursting in her mind like forsythia buds on the first warm day of the year. Then her face became troubled at a thought to which the others had led, and which she felt it best to express thus:

'Then there was that shocking day when the engine driver stopped his train and threw pieces of track aggregate at you, an innocent child! Who could wonder if from that moment we dated your attitude towards authority? Such a thing could hardly fail to influence the pattern of a young child's future growth, could it? This is an example of the importance to them of geography: who could guess such a start without knowing that we had once lived in a house so near the railway?'

The old lady paused for effect, made it, carried on:

'It was I who first told you the comic story of God, remember, which will no doubt be passed on to readers in due course.'

Christie's mother paused again. It was time to end while she was still at a fastigium, she thought: and so recommenced:

'We fondly believe that there is going to be a reckoning, a day upon which all injustices are evened out, when what we have done will beyond doubt be seen to be right, when the light of our justification blazes forth upon the world. But we are wrong: learn, then, that there is not going to be any day of reckoning, except possibly by accident. It seems that enough accidents happen for it to be a hope or even an expectation for most of us, the day of reckoning. But we shall die untidily, when we did not properly expect it, in a mess, most things unresolved, unreckoned, reflecting that it is all chaos. Even if we understand that all is chaos, the understanding itself represents a denial of chaos, and must therefore be an illusion.'

Christie's mother paused for the last time after this weighty and inelegant piece of dialectic; then concluded:

'My welcome is outstayed. I have lived as much of my life as I wish. It is simply time to go. We all have to go, though we have all been told so too many times. I cannot say I am really content: who could? But I do accept. And even without opening the reserve stock of tinned goods there is sufficient food to last you two or perhaps three days if my death should cause you any loss of appetite. The house is yours. The money in my savings book will bury me decently, if decency is what you decide matters. The rest you must take in the state of chaos in which I found it, and in which I leave it.'

Christie's mother died.

CHAPTER IV

In which a Goat is Succoured

'Why is a funeral necessary?' asked Christie.

'It is customary,' said the Undertaker.

'I know it is customary,' said Christie, 'but why is it necessary?'

'It has always gone on,' replied the Undertaker, 'and it always will go on.'

I wish I were capable of such faith, thought Christie. And he will have to sue me for his account. What can he do if I refuse to pay? Were my mother not being cremated, he could threaten to dig her up again. As it is, he is perhaps limited to doing something unpleasant with her ashes.

Christie was the only mourner, economy as to relatives (as to so many other things) being one of the virtues of this novel. The Reverend paid to perform the ceremony sang lustily and unembarrassed by himself (he had done it before) to Christie's uncomfortable stare. The coffin slid jerkily away through the low oak doors bound for the NTGB holocaust. As Christie turned into the aisle and went towards the door it was to find that the Reverend had doubled round through some back passage quickly enough to be able to offer his condolences to the departing bereaved. Christie remembered his fee at this point; that is, he remembered that the Undertaker's estimate had included a fee for the Reverend. Christie smiled at the thought that the Reverend mistakenly thought he was going to be paid. The Reverend, encouraged of course, smiled back and pressed into Christie's hand, by way of valediction, a leaflet.

When my time comes, thought Christie, if it ever does . . .

Christie gave directions to his Undertaker that the single wreath was to be disposed of by being offered not to a hospital but to the nearest branch of the People's Dispensary for Sick Animals (if it was still called that) there to be fed if possible to a sphacelated goat. The Undertaker solemnly undertook responsibility for the execution of this last request of Christie's mother, who had been unreasonably fond of goats.

The Reverend's leaflet was a Newsletter to all those (both of them? thought Christie) who worshipped regularly at the Anglican church of St Jude, Hammersmith. Christie read it, on the sofa that was now his, when he reached home, noting how heedless was the Reverend in his too frequent use of the typewriter exclamation mark formed (unsatisfactorily) by an apostrophe over a full stop. There were also a number of spelling and grammatical errors for which Christie forgave the Reverend. Then he went over to the bureau that was also now his, took out some lilac notepaper and wrote the following letter to the Borough of Hammersmith Weights and Measures Department:

28 Mall Road
London W6

Dear Sirs:
re St Jude's Church
You will note that the organisation publishing the

enclosed leaflet claims to have 'the answer to all problems, personal, political and international.'

I would be grateful if you would check upon the factual accuracy of this claim and, if you find it to be in any way false or exaggerated, I trust you will institute proceedings under the relevant section of the Trade Descriptions Act.

Yours sincerely,
Christie Malry

CHAPTER V

The Duel of Dictionary Words Between
Skater and Wagner; and the
Revelation of the Latter's Nickname

I shall now attempt a little dialogue between Christie and the Office Supervisor, as if it had happened.

SUPERVISOR: Malry, I've asked you . . .

CHRISTIE: Mr Malry, please. Or Christie, if you like. It's up to you.

SUPERVISOR: Who is interviewing who?

CHRISTIE: 'Friendly chat' was your very expression.

SUPERVISOR: A form of words. Malry, I cannot say that . . .

CHRISTIE: Mr Malry, I must insist. Or Christie. People from the earliest times have been strict about forms of address. You are attacking me by calling me names. I refer you to other wars. Call me by my proper name.

There was silence. On either side, in balance, were the power to sack, and the power to resign. It was not a time for the former, the Supervisor decided. He would not call him anything.

SUPERVISOR: Where were you yesterday afternoon?

CHRISTIE: At my mother's funeral.

SUPERVISOR: Why didn't you ask permission?

CHRISTIE: She died at very short notice. In fact, with no notice at all, on the evening before last.

SUPERVISOR: Long enough for you to arrange the funeral for the next day?

CHRISTIE: There wasn't any more time. It's a short novel.

And Christie shrugged his way out, knowing there was no answer to that.

Yet as he made his way back to his Section Christie was annoyed that his Supervisor had been so unfeeling and unsympathetic about his mother's death. The Supervisor had no doubt seen himself as being professional, businesslike, standing no nonsense from death and suchlike. I have been Debited, thought Christie, Double-Entry must apply.

It was not until well on into the morning that this particular Debit could be balanced. One of Christie's more menial tasks was to open his Section's post in the mornings, and this he had done as usual, sorting it into orders, invoices and enquiries/complaints. The complaints were what gave him most pleasure to read. On this particular day there was the latest in a festering series of letters from a restaurateur who had been unlucky in the roulette of Tapper's stock rotation policy: cakes he had been sent were not only stale but vermiferous as well. The reputation of Skater's Restaurant had suffered as a result, Mr Skater maintained, and he was demanding vengeance: the first of his letters had indeed gone so far as to make the hackneyed request for the Managing Director's head under separate cover from an abject apology and an immediate settlement of untold damages. Today's letter, Christie had noted with some disappointment, evinced a certain falling-off in the quality of the Skater invective. It gave details of that small proportion of the offending goods as had escaped consumption, and the control numbers of all the batches from the trays; then it resorted anticlimactically to obfuscation as to the exact nature of what would happen if Tapper's highest authority was not on the phone apologising that very morning.

Christie removed the letter!

Christie searched his wastepaper basket, found the Skater's Restaurant envelope and removed that, too!

No one was watching.

Carefully casual, Christie Malry replaced the letter in the envelope, left it for a minute, slipped it on to his lap, left it a minute, took out his handkerchief, covered the letter, slid them both into his lefthand trouser pocket. The letter burned there in the well-known fashion all the rest of the morning. He will not ring this morning, Skater, thought Christie.

Down by the river at Hammersmith Bridge, legally in his lunch hour, Christie fed the birds with hamfat torn from the quarter he bought at the narrow shop next to the cinema in the Broadway. The lean he ate. Sparrows there were on the roof of a houseboat moored by the wall, pigeons on the paving, and gulls in the air, wheeling and screaming, *gwylan* to wail, as is their way, I repeat myself. Greasily his fingers also tore the Skater letter into many pieces, and over half an hour he released them on the ebb tide to float down past Harrods' Depository, Grosvenor Bridge, Bugsby's Reach, Frog Island and all those other evocative points.

It was a real end for them, the pieces.

Skater has left it until after his lunchtime trade has exhausted itself, thought Christie, just as I thought. Every time the phone rang Christie expected it to be Mr Skater. At ten past three it was, and he did not want to bother with such as Christie: he wanted the Managing Director. Christie gave him his Section Head, Mr Wagner. Already Christie knew Wagner's familiar name, Wanker. So great was Mr Skater's anger that his words could be distinctly heard by Christie, and without effort. He began by asking why no action had been taken on his letter. Wagner told him no letter had been received. To make sure of this the Section Head came over to Christie's desk and searched it thoroughly; then he pursued the search on the desks of two other clerks, his secretary, his assistant and his deputy. Try down at Coldharbour Point, thought Christie, with some pleasure, or even Foulness.

Skater's assertive roar when he was told that no letter had arrived could be heard several more desks away; his proposal was that (if he were there) he would defenestrate Wagner. Christie's Section Head was riled at this, and, forgetting he was putting the company's reputation in jeopardy, he suggested that were Skater to come within a hundred yards of him he would (before he could carry out his threat) be subjected to a rapid process of trituration. Skater responded with a distinctly unfair (for it was accurate) divination, from Wagner's telephone manner, of the Section Head's helminthoid resemblances. Wagner snapped back with the only word he could think of at the time, cryptorchid, though as he had never had the necessary opportunity of observing, let alone carrying out a count, Christie felt that his superior had compromised his integrity at this point. And with sounds of gulping incapacitation at both ends of the line the conversation lapsed without any sign of an eirenicon.

Christie did enjoy it all!

When Christie arrived back in Mall Road he was pleased to see he could think of it as finally his home, for there was one letter on the mat and it was addressed to him. An organisation was hoping to sell him some bulbs, flower bulbs, begged him for his attention, enclosed a reply-paid envelope. Christie felt slightly Debited at the waste of his time, and promptly Credited himself by sealing the envelope without putting anything in it and going out at once to post it.

When he came back he cooked for himself a full frying pan of onions and sausages.

Then Christie began to draw up his Accounts!

THE FIRST
RECKONING

Note that the nearer you can place the creditor to his debtor the
nicer it will look, though it does not really matter; yet, because of
an entry of a different date which is sometimes placed between the
first and the second entries where it does not look well, no little
trouble is caused in searching for them, as he who has tried knows;
but one cannot speak fully of this here, and you must help yourself
by making use of your own natural ingenuity.

Pacioli

The figures in these accounts represent a scale of values and not any specific currency.

		DR AGGRAVATION					CR RECOMPENSE		
Oct	1	Unpleasantness of Bank General Manager	1	00	Oct Apl	–	Small kindnesses from Joan	0	28
Oct Apl	–	Branch atmosphere, as described	4	50	May	1	Scratch on facade of Edwardian Office Block	0	05
Oct Apl	–	Specific lambastings from Chief and Assistant Accountants	2	30	May	2	Undertaker's bill unpaid	1	71
Nov	24	Virtually forced to join Staff Association	0	60	May	2	Letter to Weights and Measures re St Jude's	0	04
Oct Apl	–	Chagrin at learning no secrets	0	55	May	3	Destruction of Skater's letter	6	00
May	1	Restriction of movement due to Edwardian Office Block	0	05	May	3	Bulb firm's reply-paid envelope returned empty	0	03
May	2	Suffering and loss due to Undertaker	1	71	May	3	Balance owing to Christie carried forward to next Reckoning	8	67
May	2	Unpleasantness felt by presence of Reverend	0	04					
May	3	Office Supervisor's lack of sympathy	6	00					
May	3	Bulb importuning	0	03					
			16	78				16	78

CHAPTER VI

Christie Described; and the Shrike Created

An attempt should be made to characterise Christie's appearance. I do so with diffidence, in the knowledge that such physical descriptions are rarely of value in a novel. It is one of the limitations; and there are so many others. Many readers, I should not be surprised to learn if appropriate evidence were capable of being researched, do not read such descriptions at all, but skip to the next dialogue or more readily assimilable section. Again, I have often read and heard said, many readers apparently prefer to imagine the characters for themselves. That is what draws them to the novel, that it stimulates their imagination! Imagining my characters, indeed! Investing them with characteristics quite unknown to me, or even at variance with such description as I have given! Making Christie fair when I might have him dark, for an instance, a girl when I have shown he is a man? What writer can compete with the reader's imagination!

Christie is therefore an average shape, height, weight, build, and colour. Make him what you will: probably in the image of yourself. You are allowed complete freedom in the matter of warts and moles, particularly; as long as he has at least one of either.

Nor are his motives important. Especially are his motives of no importance to us, though the usual clues will certainly be given. We are concerned with his actions. A man may be defined through his actions, you will remember. We may guess at his motives, of course; he may do so as well. We may also guess at the winner of the three-fifteen at the next meeting at Market Rasen.

But Christie's girlfriend! I shall enjoy describing her! Come along, what's your name, let's have your name.
It'll come, like everything else. Try.   Where does she work?   In a butcher's, say.   She could be called the Shrike, then. Which will be too obvious to some, too obscure to others.   Ah.

CHAPTER VII

The Shrike's Two Rules; and other Observables

'Every Debit must have its corresponding Credit,' explained Christie, 'Perhaps every bad must have its corresponding good. An extension might be called Moral Double-Entry. In eating these beef olives, which is very good for us, we are at the same time preventing someone else from eating them; which is undoubtedly bad for them.'

'We had beef olives over today,' said the Shrike, 'that's why we're eating them.'

'Not in Cawnpore,' said Christie.

'Eh?' said the Shrike. 'Mr Cameron took some home, too, we had so many over.'

'Did he pay for them?' asked Christie.

'No, of course not. It's his business,' said the Shrike, without offence.

'That's an added complication,' said Christie. 'Who do we Debit? And who Credit?'

'Christ knows,' said the Shrike.

'I'm uncertain, too,' said Christie.

Here is Heisenberg's Principle of Uncertainty:

*Accurate measurement of an observable
quantity necessarily produces uncertainties*

*in one's knowledge of the values of other
observables.*

'I think he'll give up the beef olives soon,' said the Shrike,
'no one seems to want them very much any more. Only the
old people buy them now. The housewives don't know what
they are.'

'Why should they?' said Christie, 'Debit beef olives, Credit
housewives.'

'Can't you leave your work at work?' said the Shrike,
gently.

Christie nearly asked her what his work was; but he realised
he might go too far. No one must know of his Great Idea, not
even the Shrike.

The Shrike was a kindly, warm girl of about twenty-nine
whom Christie had met at the Hammersmith Palais (venerated
for the visit of the Original Dixieland Jazz Band) the night
after doing his accounts. The Shrike had picked on Christie for
a Ladies' Invitation, and that was that. Christie was not
unwilling, for the Shrike was nice, nice was the word that
applied nicely to the Shrike. Soon Christie knew that the
Shrike had an Old Mum up in Islington, that she was not
trying to find a husband like all the other girls were, that she
had a modest flat of her own in Brook Green, near splendid
Lyons' (Tapper's opposition), and that she would quite like to
see Christie again, if it suited him, she would not want to
impose but she did like his average kind face, and the way he
dressed, and the way he held her properly, and this was a
Ladies' Invitation after all, wasn't it?

'Yes,' Christie had said, generally, to everything, and thought
to himself that if he could satisfactorily stabilise his sexual

arrangements then he could the more efficiently concentrate on his Great Idea. And so it was to be: nothing happens by accident in this novel. Or almost nothing.

The occasion of the beef olives above was the second visit that Christie had made to the Shrike's flat. The first had been after the encounter at the Palais, when the Shrike had made it clear (in the same breath as she had suggested a second) that she never let anyone on the first occasion: it was one of her little rules.

After dinner on this second occasion, then, Christie having expressed proper gratitude for the provender provided, the Shrike asked him if he would care to recline on the moderately elegant sofa which helped to fill her living-room. Christie did so care, and the Shrike accordingly went to fetch her Goblin cylinder vacuum cleaner which was an old model but recently serviced and creating an excellent suction at its nozzle. The Shrike removed Christie's clothing, article by article, whilst at the same time giving him a good going over with the Goblin, using the full range of accessories as well as simply the end of the tube or pipe. Christie was enchanted: he quickly had one ejaculation, and another came after about twenty minutes. He was only eighteen. Then the Shrike took her own clothes off, very unashamedly and naturally, of course, and performed an unsophisticated but infinitely alluring dance for Christie, especially for him, solely for him. This spontaneous dance brought her closer and closer to Christie over a period of about fifteen minutes until it was being performed on top of him with extremely pleasurable results for both of them: and in the pleasantest course of time Christie and the Shrike were able to enjoy almost simultaneous orgasms of unforgettable proportions and intensities.

Now there is something on which the reader may exercise his imagination!

Afterwards they both lay for a long time on the sofa, together in body only, their minds away in different directions.

The Shrike was rehearsing in her mind how to rid herself of all other romantic and sexual encumbrances in order that she might be able to devote her full attentions to Christie. She was a good manageress, the Shrike, despite being paid only as an assistant.

Christie was considering the application of Double-Entry to sexual pleasure. He had, he soon realised, only one instrument with which to make entries: conversely, the Shrike had, in common with most women, at least three points at which entry was possible. Christie permutated the possibilities in his mind, and then mentioned them to the Shrike. To her credit, she did not then treat him as someone in whom the beast had gained the upper hand. Two she would have but the third was her own, she maintained stoutly, inviolate. It was the second of her little rules: the last is yet to come.

Christie had discovered, early on, an area in which the writ of Double-Entry did not run.

She was a real girl, the Shrike, she had hair in her armpits.

CHAPTER VIII

Christie and the Nutladies, amongst others

... the bad habit of suffering injustice in silence ...
Brecht

Christie at the office again, next day. Yesterday there was a Skaterless silence, today a letter from Skater's solicitors, not from Skater. Christie passed it straight to Wagner: not without thought.

Here is something like what Christie thought: *It goes on, then, does it? I have exacerbated, I am building up too great a Credit, if I am not careful I shall owe Tapper's a debt, I shall be overdrawn. . . . But there are all the other things Tapper's have done to me, starting with the wages they pay me, pitifully small, pitifully. This needs thinking about, accounting for, properly, when I have time. . . .*

As he took the letter, Wagner tensed a little, waved Christie away with the other hand. There was no sign that he knew Christie had removed the earlier letter: how could there have been? But Christie was apprehensive just the same. He knew they could not prove he took it: but he himself knew. He also felt a slight disappointment that they did not know he knew. He would have enjoyed his Credit more if he had known that they knew. Perhaps.

At eleven or thereabouts Christie was told by Wagner to go over to Wages Section and fill a void there for the rest of the day or however long they needed him, whichever were to prove the shorter. Parsons of Wages was down with a head cold, streaming nose, inflated adenoids; a sad, serious case. Christie's job in Parsons' absence was to carry heavy box trays of wage packets (it being payday) round successive departments of the Factory and the Bakery. With him to pay out, guide, instruct and entertain was Headlam, Bedlam to his friends at school, no joke now.

'What exactly do they do in Nutcrackers?' asked Christie, 'I've wondered for some days now, seeing the name in the internal phone list.'

'There are eight of them,' replied the affable Headlam, 'and a Forelady. You'll see. The Forelady sits at a small table in the centre of the room, and she hits a nut with her little nut-hammer. Then the other eight scuttle round the floor looking for the kernel.'

When they arrived at Nutcrackers there were indeed nine ladies present, but all of them had one or another form of nucifrage and all of them had nuts of various kinds in front of them on their own tables. When the Wages Men entered a cheer went up, part ironic, part relieved, part sexual challenge. The presence of Christie caused much excitement, and one lady threw an accurate filbert which bounced on his tray before clipping his average diaphragm.

'Nutladies, nutladies, please!' shouted Headlam. 'Mr Parsons is unfit for play this week because of the inevitable groin strain, and in his place, making his home debut, is our young Mr Christie Malry!'

The Nutladies ooed and aahed, and two commented on the probable size of Christie's unmentionables. They clustered round as Headlam produced his key to unlock the box tray that hung from Christie's neck, but the Forelady chivvied them into a line and one by one they took the proffered packet with one hand and groped with the other beneath the tray for Christie's aforeunmentionables. Christie yelped the first twice and then evaded the others by bending at the neck and causing the heavy tray to lever on each a forearm. All in good part the Nutladies took it, none of them under fifty.

The Forelady was last to receive her packet, then took Headlam aside for a private word: and something changed hands, one of Headlam's jacket pockets bulged. Christie too was offered a nut, by a coquette of fifty-four, blushed, accepted, and the cheer went up again as they left.

'Every Department has its speciality,' advised Headlam, 'no one is the same as any other.'

From the ground floor Nutladies they next visited the subterranean Boilermen who stoked the fire and provided the power that kept the whole of Tapper's turning over at the top of the catering tree. A very different reception here, confirmation: the Boilermen were subdued, did not turn from their harsh work. The noise was so great as to be physically oppressive. Headlam led the way past one great boiler, then another, to a small office in one corner formed of steel partitions. In there the noise was slightly less noticeable. The foreman nodded at Headlam, ignored Christie, and took all his Department's wage packets out in a vast handful. He came part of the way back with them, stopping to call a Boilerman over about a query on last week's wage stoppages which Headlam dealt with courteously and efficiently. Christie tired of holding the heavy box tray while he was waiting, and looked round for somewhere to set it down for a moment. There were some large steel terminal and junction boxes fixed to the wall, and

Christie moved across to use them as suitable ledges on which to rest the weight. Just as he was about to do so, the Foreman called sharply across to him:

'Watch it, son, or the whole of Tapper's will grind to a standstill!'

Christie moved away as though the boxes had had exterior and live terminals about to reach out and electrocute him. As he did so, it occurred to him that should Tapper's ever Debit him sufficiently he now had the knowledge (if not yet the means) by which a massive Credit might be exacted.

And as he and Headlam made their rewarding pilgrimage about Tapper's alimentary empire, more and more Christie realised what an opportunity he was being given: a guided tour of the enemy defences, a chance to observe weaknesses and strong points, vulnerable outposts and key redoubts, salients and bridgeheads, and similar war-game expressions. Was this a war? Was this a game?

After Fancy Goods, Fondant, and Maintenance Departments, Headlam and Christie had to go back to the Wages Section for another box tray. They took this first to the basement (Headlam had worked out a weight/load itinerary which he claimed was both the most economical and ergonomically sound that could be devised) where four great machines were relatively slowly going DOOM, DOOM, DOOM, DOOM, as if in imitation of the marine engines in that MacNeice poem. Christie saw that the machines consisted of a central shaft which eccentrically drove two opposed and paddle-ended connecting-rods. The paddles each puddled a muddy brown viscous liquid: Christie knew by the colour it must be milk one end, plain the other.

A ventripotent Foreman expanded towards them:

'Hallo, DOOM, who's DOOM this, DOOM Head DOOM lam DOOM eh? DOOM'

'Mr DOOM Malry DOOM Tiny DOOM Mr DOOM Parsons DOOM is DOOM . . .'

That is enough of that, certainly. Let us subside with relief into *oratio obliqua*.

Niceties over, Tiny explained to Christie that all chocolate had to take a two days' thumping to and fro in these machines to qualify as superfine: night and day, DOOM DOOM! went his worshipped machines down here in their basement, DOOM DOOM. Christie could see the sheen of professional passion in Tiny's eyes as he savoured the bashing the baths of chocolate took. And he was not slow in indicating his favourite, either, Tiny: the dark brown bath, and he explained that this was the only real tipple, all the other seven being milk. Seeing a sadness overcome him, Christie asked the reason, and soon knew it. There were those to whom it was given to like plain chocolate, said Tiny, the connoisseurs, the cognoscenti, the true aristocrats; and there were the rest, the others, the chocolate *lumpen-proletariat*. The observant will be aware that I have avoided a claret-burgundy comparison here, having an unashamed preference for the latter myself (when I can afford either) and use of the cliché *crème de la crème* was also rejected for its punning awkwardness.

Tiny kept a Georgian handled gill glass by this one royal bath, and from this he periodically (he told them) supped his beloved nectar to ascertain whether or not it had reached its apogee. A fortunate man, thought Christie; and it crossed his mind that the right kind of foreign body in the bath could well yield a handsome Credit.

From this Department Headlam's itinerary more or less chronologically followed the manufacturing process, at least on the confectionery side. Christie was as near overawed as may be by the great vats and cauldrons of the Sugar Boilers, for instance, and saw that a great deal of chaos, injury and possibly loss of life, too, could be occasioned by a certain type of accident in this Department. Christie drew back at the thought of loss of life, however: the contra entry to that one could only be, he thought at this stage, his own death.

There was less that was interesting from the Double-Entry point of view in the Moulders and Enrobers Department. The whole of one floor was divided approximately in half by a series of vertical grilles down which molten chocolate poured. Through this viscoid curtain passed a horizontal travelling belt of wire mesh bearing small moulded shapes. On one side of the room these shapes, the soft or hard centres of chocolates, were moulded in great dinted trays. The colours were unappealing to Christie: perhaps that is why they cover them, he thought. As the centres came through the enrobing fall of chocolate, girls on either side of the belt added the finishing and distinctive decoration: it looked highly skilled, the artful forming of the soft top coating into an arabesque, a coil, a leaf – but mindlessly monotonous for those doing it, Christie thought. Here there were one or two attractive girls, but they could not look up at the Wages Men for fear of missing a chocolate and having it end up as a rejected misshape farther down the line. The Forewoman marched up and down at the ends of the belts, supervising the loading of trays on to trolleys, checking the percentages of misshapes. She hardly stopped to take charge of her Department's packets; but she did slip Headlam and

66

Christie a bag each of misshapes of their own before virtually dismissing them.

They ate them on their way to the Boxmakers. Here the machinery looked clean and somehow dry, though sweetly lubricated, and it ticked and chattered rather than thundered. The floor was dusty with strawboard litter; scraps of card and ribbon were everywhere, whilst great stacks of board filled a third of the workroom. The atmosphere was as that of a medieval craft guild shop might have been, quaint and yet efficient: no better ways had been found of making boxes, so they used much the same methods and machinery as had been used for centuries to score and square and cut. At Tapper's, anyway.

The Foreman of the Boxmakers fitted this setting exactly, was perhaps its present architect: he was tall, thin, about fifty, quietly assured, and easy in his command. He invited the Wages Men into his tidy little office, discussed football without rancour, drew their attention to this new month's nude on his calendar, expressed the opinion that she would be worth their while coming back to see, next week, when they might, if they thought of it, if it was not too much trouble, of course, that was well understood, bring the wages with them.

Christie was charmed by the man, but some of the while he was watching points, Christie, of course: paper, card, could be made to burn!

The box trays were empty: Headlam and Christie made their way back to Wages Section yet again. Headlam gave some misshapes to Lucy, the girl on the top desk, and offered some to Stegginson, his Section Head.

'I wouldn't eat this firm's muck if you paid me!' said Stegginson violently.

'He always says that,' said Headlam to Christie.

'How many rats did you see today?' Stegginson went on, 'leaping in and out of those baths in the basement? I've seen them the size of terriers! Terriers! Chocolate-coated terrier-rats, a new line, go down a treat at the Savoy they do! Can't get enough of them! Ha!'

Christie did not know whether to laugh or not; indeed, he did not quite know whether he found it funny or not.

'He's always like that,' said Lucy.

'There you are,' said Headlam. 'What did I say?'

Stegginson retired to his desk, half hidden by steel cupboards and a filing cabinet.

'As Parsons is away,' he said, suddenly reappearing, 'You and Lucy can't take your lunch hour together.'

'Okay, Lucy, d'you want to go first?' asked Headlam, and Christie saw at once that there was more than a working relationship between them.

'No,' she said, and smiled, 'I'll finish this off. You go, I'll go when you come back.'

So Headlam and Christie had lunch in the Eel and Pie Shop on the curve by Hammersmith flyover, and very cheaply and nourishingly too. Headlam had eels, carefully sucking the clinging flesh from the awkward bone and genteelly removing it afterwards. Christie could not fancy the eels, but had double pie, double mash and double liquor instead. The thick parsleyed liquor he sharpened with plenty of vinegar, and savoured the blend thus made with the crude pastry and tasty meat contained in it. I must bring the Shrike here, thought Christie, since I enjoy it I am sure she would, too.

While they ate, Headlam told Christie true stories of Tapper's. Of how they had bought from Switzerland an especially sophisticated machine for wrapping chocolate bars, which had arrived in an enormous packing case. In order to install this in the basement the Tapper's Governors had said, We shall have to make a big hole in the ground floor and lower it through. When they had with infinite trouble cut the hole they opened the huge case and found that the machine had been packed unassembled, was in small parts which could each have easily been carried by one man down the stairs. Christie laughed quite a lot at this.

'They were even more clever over the Bakery,' said Headlam of the Tapper's Governors, again, 'which is a newer building than the Factory. You'll see it this afternoon. It's laid out with each different Department having a floor to itself, and they became so involved with the proper layout of each floor that they forgot to put any stairs in.'

Headlam saw Christie's disbelief.

'No, it's true,' said Headlam. 'The stairs were an afterthought. You have a look this afternoon. They were just stuck on the outside.'

Christie accepted that the Tapper's Governors were stupid: how did they come to be rich, he wondered? And then he wondered aloud to Wages Headlam how much the Governors actually received by way of recompense for their stupidity.

'I know or can find out how much anyone in the Factory or the Bakery takes home,' said Headlam, 'and Wages Section, in the delectable person of Lucy, also deals with Office wages. But only up to the level of Section Heads. The Governors are dealt with by the Chief Accountant personally, monthly and by bank transfer. And here is something you will find difficult to believe, Christie, about Lucy and the Office Wages Slips. Now I am excessively loose with Lucy, I fuck her from arsehole to breakfast as often as may be, which is several times a week, and indeed I often wonder which flat it is I spend more time in, hers or mine, and no doubt in the fullness of Tapper's time we shall qualify for one of their wedding cakes; which is to say that I love and am grossly intimate with this lovely Wages Girl, yet do you know that when I enquire of her, out of casual interest, how much the Head of the Typing Pool, say, receives by way of emolument, she will not tell me? Would you credit it?'

'I'd have to think about it,' said Christie.

'She is most stubbornly Puritan about this one thing. She has loyalty to some concept of Tapper's which I cannot understand. She has been bought, and that is that. In all else, especially sexually, she is most definitely not Puritan. Her reticence in this matter is the only thing that makes me have doubts about making her mine forever.'

Headlam sighed, pushed his plate away from him and, seeing Christie had finished too, stood up to go. On the way back, still having half their lunch hour to themselves, he suggested they have a drink in the Long Bar. Christie wondered about the wisdom of this, of going back to breathe stout all over his Section Head: but then recollected that he was on loan to Wages and it was the Bakery staff who would benefit, not Wagner. So he enjoyed a pint of Guinness with Headlam, both being slumped against the counter.

'I'm twenty-nine,' said Headlam, 'and I've worked for Tapper's since I was twenty. In that time my salary has just about kept pace with the cost of living. I am at a standstill, except when I am with lovely Lucy. If Stegginson dropped dead tomorrow I should be in line for his job. I could do it with the greatest of ease. So can he. I shall be forty-seven when he retires. If I stay, if I live. I like it this way, I'm happy, I have all I want.'

In Wages Section Stegginson picked up the phone as soon as Headlam and Christie arrived back, spoke briefly into it, and then nodded to them. Headlam explained that one day one of the Governors had seen from his eyrie a couple of men who might or might not have been ill-intentioned loitering outside Tapper's. They had been in a position to have interfered, had they so wished, with the Wages Men as they made their encumbered way along the road between the Factory and the Bakery, and to have helped themselves to a number, if not all, of the wage packets in the two box trays, again if they had been so minded. No men, or women, had so far been so minded, but the Governors' natural caution had thenceforward dictated that the Wages Men would proceed the seventy or so yards from Factory to Bakery in a securely-locked motor vehicle provided by Transport Section. It was this that Stegginson had just summoned. Christie wondered why the Factory and the Bakery were not connected internally, but from what Headlam had told him about the Bakery stairs he assumed he could guess the answer to any question he might ask; and saved it.

The Bakery was of course something different for Christie after the wide variety of the Factory. On the ground and first floors most of the space was taken up with great long ovens, like marine boilers, with cast-iron doors. The men wore chef's tall hats and the women wore white muslin squares tying their hair out of sight and the cakes. They all lined up for their wages silently, some of them proudly. Christie noted where the switches were, the heat regulators for the massive ovens.

On the two floors above the mixtures to feed these ovens

were prepared. Two women appeared to be employed solely cutting lemons in half and squeezing out the juice. They were extremely deft, each half-lemon being wrung out with a single thrusting, twisting movement on a campaniform metal mould. Elsewhere great stainless steel agitators pounded doughs and cakemixes eccentrically and endlessly within detachable bowls on castors.

Christie saw nothing unhygienic or dirty enough to explain Stegginson's outburst. Indeed, on the top floor of the Bakery the general impression combined something of the cleanliness of a laboratory with the quiet dedication of an artists' atelier. Here was the Wedding and Speciality Cake Department, the sculptors with the icing nozzle; here they could turn out a seven-tier tower for a Lord Mayor's Banquet, or an exact miniature of the third act set to celebrate the first year of a successful West End run, and Xmas cakes that brought to mind the excesses of Dickens. Ah. Here they even wore different headgear, too, both men and women having a white linen version of a Rembrandt cap, to show they were indubitably artists. Their behaviour bore this out, being apparently casual and inconsidered rather than plodding or frenetic like the other workers below.

Headlam made his way amongst them, greeting most by name, respectful and friendly. Many of the icers barely looked up from their engrossing work, so apparently careless were they of being paid. One fat, dumpy lady of about forty-five, however, was jollied out of her absorption by the physical attentions of Headlam, who put his arm round her, squeezed, then took her warm, icy hand and pressed into it her weekly due, the while saying:

'How are you, Flossie, my love, my only treasure? Christie,

this is Flossie, who's going to ice my lucky Lucy's lovely wedding cake just as soon as she's qualified for one. And you know what it's going to be, don't you, darling?'

'Remind me again,' said Flossie, 'or, what is it this week, darling?'

'A prick rampant, my love,' said Headlam, 'and crossed balls, gules, on a stormy sea of pubic hair, argent. What else is appropriate for nuptials?'

Flossie waved a thumb, indicating a stock cupboard with a glass front.

'Horseshoes,' she said, 'and bride-and-grooms hand-in-hand, bells, vicars, churches in assorted architectural styles, old boots, tin cans, hearts, hearts, hearts.'

'Not very artistic,' said Headlam.

'Then you shall have it,' said Flossie.

'When?' said Headlam.

'Aha!' said Flossie.

Headlam kissed her on the cheek and then moved Christie away towards the Icing Foreman's office, saying as they went:

'In five months my Lucy will have been here three years, which means that she will then qualify for a wedding cake, gratis with the compliments of the Tapper's Governors, on the occasion of her marriage. So then the pressure will be on, boy, then the moment of truth regarding how much the Office Supervisor takes home will be upon us!'

The Icing Foreman's office on this floor was carpeted, quiet, deep in luxury, but combining a functional aspect rather like the captain's quarters on a cruise liner. Headlam sank into a huge leather pouffe, Christie sat on one end of a sofa, and the Icing Foreman served them both with strong cold cocktails of his own devising in glasses frosted at the top with sugar. Then he and Headlam discussed the state of the share market in serious, hushed voices.

After about ten minutes the phone rang. The Icing Foreman answered it, and Christie heard Stegginson at the other end, in a voice clearly meant to be loud enough to overhear, say:

'Has that bugger Headlam reached you yet, Alan?'

'No sign of him yet, George,' said the Icing Foreman ritually, 'Any message?'

'Tell him I'll knot his cock for him when he gets back, Alan, if you will.'

'Okay, George,' said the Icing Foreman, then put down the phone and continued his conversation with Headlam as though nothing had happened.

Christie loved it all! The thought that Tapper's might be a microcosm crossed his mind: to be allowed to continue into limbo as being unworthy of him. From the windows of this top floor he could see the Roumieu-Gough-Seddon tower of St Paul's Parish Church, the four gilded French-pavilion finials of Hammersmith Bridge, and the subtile curve of the flyover. Farther round there was Manbré & Garton's Sugar Refinery, a shared interest. It was all so pleasant with another cocktail in his hand, that Christie forgot for a moment to look for ways in which future Credits might possibly be established. The corruption of it! So he steeled himself to ignore the conversation and the view, and he looked coldly around him. He found one way quite quickly: on the wall outside the office were some fire extinguishers of the dry powder type. One of those let loose at random in this white ice environment, considered Christie, would render much technically inedible under the various Pure Food and Drug Acts! And, delighted that he had discharged his duty, Christie settled back to enjoy his third cocktail, his second and more careful view.

Then again the phone rang and Stegginson was loud at either end.

'Ah!' lied the Icing Foreman to him. 'They've just walked in!'

'Liar,' said Stegginson, 'Put him on to me.'

Headlam finished his drink, refilled his glass from the shaker and added an extra couple of cubes of ice. He picked up the phone, and before answering swallowed loudly, clinked the ice in the glass as near as possible to the mouthpiece, and then belched just loud enough to be heard.

'Headlam!' shouted Stegginson, 'I know what you're doing!'

'No you don't,' said Headlam, sawing at his crotch with the index finger extended from the hand holding his glass.

'You bugger, Headlam! Ten minutes I'll give you to get back here, ten minutes!'

'If you want the Bakery Round done quicker, you old goat, you order yourself to do it!' said Headlam, and clinked the ice in his glass again.

'I'll tie a running bowline in it for you, bugger you!'

'You need two ends for that one, I think,' said Headlam, belched again but more loudly, and put the phone down.

'Perhaps he'll use yours too, for the bowline,' he said to Christie as he went back to his pouffe. 'What's this new girl like, Alan? She must be something special or you wouldn't have started her at two points up from basic.'

'Straight out of Pastry School,' said Alan, 'a technical virgin but already a virtuoso with the nozzle, would you credit it?'

Christie thought about that one.

And so it went on for another half hour. At length Headlam

heaved himself sideways off the pouffe on to the floor, crouched a moment, then sprang upright.

'Off!' he said to Christie, 'or Stegginson will be annoyed. Cheers, Alan.'

Stegginson stayed silent and unseen behind his cover when they arrived back at Wages Section.

'He's always like that,' said Headlam, 'it's guilt.'

Guilt? And Christie wondered to himself.

CHAPTER IX

A Promise Fulfilled, and Christie's
Younger Life; a Failed Chapter

Here is the story promised you on page 29, as told to Christie at his Catholic mother's shapely knee:

It seems there has always existed a God, or it may be that He created Himself. There is no doubt, however, that He claims to have created something He calls the world, though in context this must be extended to cover the universe or universes, too. Into this world He places various creations, roughly interdependent though a certain amount of jockeying for position is evident in the early stages. Amongst these creations is Man and (shortly afterwards) Woman. God gives this couple, known as Adam and Eve, something called free will, which means they can act as they like. If they act as God does not like, however, they will get thumped. It is not by any means clear what God does or does not like. The first thing Adam and Eve do is not to God's liking. It turns out that God knew this was going to happen, because He is omniscient. It also turns out that He could have stopped it, too, because He is omnipotent. Adam and Eve are of course quite baffled by what is going on, but take their thumping with reasonably good grace. They even go on to have three sons. That's that, you must be thinking, the family must die out. But no: God has been making it all up as He goes along, like certain kinds of novelist, and He promptly reveals the existence of some Tribes who have Women with whom two of the sons (one having been prematurely killed) can mate and carry on what they imagine is God's Plan for the World ... but my editor at Viking says that all this sort of thing has been done before, and at a time when it meant something, too. Certainly Rayner's re-telling was better.

My point is that when Christie first heard it he lisped:
'I believe it! I believe it all!'
As we all do at the age of two.

One would have thought that exposed to that sort of lying tale-telling any vicious development in Christie's character could only too easily be explained. But no, for almost all of his generation (and indeed every English generation) had been similarly exposed, and patently none of them had had Christie's Great Idea. We must therefore look farther than this story and the account given by Christie's mother before she left us.

From six to nine years you already know that Christie lived near a railway line. You did not until now know that it was at Tiptree, in Essex. From birth to six he lived with his mother in a converted railway (ah! already a no doubt significant conjunction!) carriage on the edge of the salt flats at Maldon, also in Essex. At nine, the closely-knit family moved to the metropolis, scenting excitement, Woolworths and the British Home Stores in King Street, Hammersmith. So Christie had become quite a globetrotter by the age of ten!

You must be curious about Christie's father. So am I.

Christie went to a Secondary School in Hammersmith. Bernie Berkovitch was his best friend. When I grow up, Bernie had told Christie, I'm going to be a traveller in ladies' underwear. When he did grow up, Bernie became a drummer in an Irish Show Band and saw his girlfriend killed in a car crash. Christie lost touch with Bernie after that, as you might expect. They were very young for such things.

The points of the compass, carried out in brass and ten feet from north to south, were let into the floor of the School Hall. The wood blocks wearing quicker than the brass, the letters and lines protruded slightly prouder each year; by the time Christie was in attendance they were sufficiently so to be the cause of several accidents each term. The Headmaster would do nothing to relieve the condition; he maintained that the object was an antique and that it did not cause accidents in any case since it was children running into it which did that. Christie himself fell over it three times, the second injuring his left knee so badly that it left his left leg a permanently twisted misshape.

Other things left other marks, too.

Piggy Webb the woodwork master cooked his lunch over the gluepot gasring, threw chisels at inattents. Mr Tripp the Welsh wizard waxed fiery every history lesson over the cunning of the English. Mecca the PE master had them all in a triangle, himself at its apex, on Parents' Day, bent at the knees, arms raised, saluting him in studied unison.... I'm going to pack this in soon: both everything and nothing in a person's past and background may be significant.

Physically Christie as an adolescent had no more than his fair share of spots and blemishes: is that significant?

Yes.

No.

Oh, I could go on and on for pages and pages about Christie's young life, inventing and observing, remembering and borrowing. But why?   All is chaos and unexplainable.   These things happened. He is as he is, you are as you are.   Act on that: all is chaos.   The end is coming, truly.

It is just so much wasted effort to attempt to understand anything.

Lots of people never had a chance, are ground down, and other clichés. Far from kicking against the pricks, they love their condition and vote conservative.

THE SECOND
RECKONING

. . . you should always see that you have proper evidence of debits and credits in the proper manner and clearness, if possible, and in the handwriting of the clerks of such places. In these offices the clerks are often changed, and each of these desires to keep the books in his own way. They always blame the previous clerks, by saying that the books have not been kept in good order, and are always persuading you to believe that their way is better than that of any of the others, and for such reason they sometimes mix up the accounts of the said offices in such a manner that they do not correspond in any way. . . .

Pacioli

		DR AGGRAVATION					CR RECOMPENSE			
May	4	Balance brought forward	8	67	May	5	Skater's legal action		1	30
May	5	Verbal aggression by			May	5	Four misshapes		0	01
		Stegginson (indirect)	0	02						
					May	31	Balance owed to Christie			
May	12	Revelation of Holy					carried forward to			
		storytelling	60	00			next Reckoning		106	61
May	19	Bernie Berkovitch's								
		trouble (indirect)	0	23						
May	31	Injury to left knee at								
		school	4	00						
May	31	General educational								
		trauma	35	00						
			107	92					107	92

CHAPTER X

Christie Codifies his Great Idea

Christie decided it was time that he codified some principles (for want of a better word) for his great idea. He took a whole weekend over it. These were the principles he thought of for himself:

1] I act alone. I do not seek the assistance of anyone else whatsoever. I carry out only such actions as are within my own capabilities. I am a cell of one.

2] It follows that I enjoy my successes (and grieve over my failures) alone. I tell no one of either; not even the Shrike.

3] My duty to myself is equally to attack and to survive to attack again.

4] I must not appear to be different in any way from those around me. I should appear satisfied with the job at which I am earning a living.

5] I do not need more money than I earn, and should not attempt projects which require more money than I ordinarily have.

6] I should not think I am cleverer than I am. After a major project I should return to minor ones.

7] Every project is important, however small.

8] I am always attacking (when I am attacking, when I am active) never defending. If I am defending, it means they know I am there to attack: which must never happen. If I am forced to defend, I am lost.

9] My chief advantage is that their system has classed me as not being clever enough to be known: to be effective, and to continue to be effective, I must preserve this unknownness next to my life.

10] While it is so important to be unknown, to be no one, from their point of view, within myself I must be constantly aware that I am not no one, that I am who I am. That is, I must hold closely to my inner knowledge of myself. If this were merely an intellectual and partial change, then I could practise holding my true self back by a change of location. That is, I could be my true self, in my own particular knowledge, reserving that self for that one place. But I cannot do this: I must be that self, as well and all the time, while I am out, at all various places, the scenes of my intended triumphs.

11] I must not be present when an action takes place. I must resist the very natural desire to be there to see it when it happens: I must be away, and hear about it, like almost everyone else, at some other hand.

12] I cannot afford to face superior odds; but I take heart from the fact that I have seen there to be innumerable occasions when the odds are quite indisputably in my favour.

Christie did not write down these principles or thoughts, as I have, for especially the Shrike had eyes.

Christie thought it was a weekend well spent, though.

CHAPTER XI

Christie Begins in Earnest; and (Something to please all Model Railway Enthusiasts) an Account of the Little Vermifuge

The most important thing is to begin, and to begin with a great spirit of decisiveness and boldness.

A Manual of Twentieth-Century Archery

A little action.

On his way home Christie saw one edge of a poster torn at a corner, pulled it circumspectly as he passed, Credited himself, Debited cigarettes, papermakers, printers, advertising agencies and the poets who worked for them.

At home, as the day waned, as it were, Christie reached out for his late mother's air pistol, loaded it, and poshed the streetlamp glass outside with only his eleventh shot.

Afterwards Christie picked up the telephone. Then he had second thoughts, and went out into Mall Road and round the corner to the pub and used the phone there. He dialled Scotland Yard and told them, in tones of great seriousness, that he had just left a bomb in the stalls of the Aldwych Theatre timed to explode in fifteen minutes. Next, the National, he thought!

But that was enough for one evening. Christie had one light ale, went home and ate sparingly, and then called by arrangement on the Shrike for a little comfort.

You should beware of concluding from the above that Christie's intention was only a little miching malicho.

Considering his future: Christie saw clearly that he should remain at Tapper's, and not seek promotion or distinction in any way. But Wagner's Section was limited in opportunities for Credits to Christie: Wages Section, he had seen, abounded in them. But how could he arrange a transfer?

Christie suggested to his new friend Headlam that they might take their respective girlfriends, the Shrike and Lucy, to the Palais the next evening. Headlam thought this an excellent idea, and suggested that they meet the girls inside: in this way, Headlam went on, they would have to pay for themselves. Or at least Lucy would.

'We're saving money to get married,' he explained.

But Christie was not as illogical as that, nor mean, nor did he have plans to marry. So he paid for his beloved Shrike and bought her a vodka and tomato juice as well, which the genteel girl referred to as a Bee Mary, eschewing coarse language.

The Shrike and Lucy took to each other, and after about an hour or so invited each other to dance: they said this was to give the men time for a drink together, but really Lucy wanted to sound out the Shrike's opinion as to the relative merits of circumcised and uncircumcised men. Christie and Headlam made for the bar, and even as the till rang the Wages Man said:

'Why don't you come and join us on wages? D'you fancy a transfer?'

Did Christie! Was Headlam clairvoyant?

'Parsons looks like being indisposed for the rest of this novel,' went on Headlam. 'In fact, I think he's just caught something fatal.'

'But what about Stegginson?' doubted Christie.

'Stegginson will do what I tell him to do,' said Headlam, 'I've got something on Stegginson which he knows I've got and I know he knows I've got. There are limits, of course, to how I can use it, but in this case Stegginson can have no objection.'

'But what about Wagner?' said Christie, leading him on.

'You'll find this difficult to believe,' said Headlam, 'until you've been at Tapper's as long as I have, but I've got something on Wanker, as well. In fact, the same thing I have on Stegginson involves your Section Head too. Besides others, and besides other things.'

'It sounds as though you run the Office,' said Christie admiringly.

'Within limits,' said Headlam, 'I do run the Orifice.'

And with that the girls rejoined them. Christie was very relaxed and relieved that an important aspect of his future had now been settled, and reminisced charmingly as he danced with the Shrike about how they had met on this very sprung floor and how everything was all right now and was going to go on being all right and would then become even better. He was very uncomplicated, Christie, and in the Shrike he had met his simple match.

There were not many causes for Debit during the first part of Christie's last week on Invoices; to create a contra entry to what few there were Christie contented himself with taking home some paper clips, a rubber stamp pad, and similar small items of stationery. But towards the end of the week, for reasons which Christie could only assume were connected with whatever hold Headlam had on Wagner, his Section Head imposed savage work burdens on him, tonguelashed him more than once unjustly, and generally Debited Christie very severely.

Christie spent the whole of one early evening trying to work out a balancing entry, time being short. It was clear to him that he could step up his transfer of stationery in volume simply by taking a briefcase or larger receptacle into the office; but there was a possibility of being caught, since Tapper's Security Section did hold random checks on departing employees to discourage the growth of a black market in smuggled walnut cakes and misshapes. Besides, there was the problem of disposing of such things as A4 bank paper, which burnt very slowly in bulk. Christie played back on the tapeheads of his mind a whole Wagner working day, determined to find a better way of squaring the accounts. Finally he stopped at the way his Section Head signed Memos and Orders, ran back, replayed it once, and twice to make sure. Then he was sure, and could turn his mind to the Shrike's delights, which included dinner.

It was another part of Christie's job at this time to collate and pass on orders, as it was of several other of his colleagues. These orders were of two categories: internal and external. The internal are what Christie was concerned with on this particular morning. The various Departments of the Factory, Bakery and Office would all make out their requirements on the standard form and send it to Wagner who would order it appropriately from an outside supplier.

Wagner signed hundreds of orders a day, actually reading perhaps one in ten.

They were good odds.

Christie took his lunch early, twelve to one, as the pattern of office routine allowed. Thus he was alone at his desk when all the others were out.

Christie went to a colleague's typewriter and sat down. Riffling through a pile of his own work, he came across an order from Sales Department for five cartons of carbon paper. Christie typed an official order for five tons of carbon paper, went back to his own desk and included the order with all the others he had done that morning, in the knowledge that Wagner's usual practice was to lift the corner of each of the pile just sufficiently to scrawl at great speed his wizened and entirely personal signature. Ah. And Christie wore gloves (rubber, of course, close-fitting, skin-coloured) the while, so that no link with him could be made. The perfect crime. You may look forward to the arrival of a lorry at Tapper's loaded with enough carbon paper to keep them going until the end of the century. For Wagner signed without noticing, as usual.

As he had some time to spare before the others came back, and his gloves still on, Christie made out some extra cards for the Calls File. This was an index system which acted as a reminder to do certain things on certain days. Each day first thing in the morning the cards for that day were taken out and acted upon. Christie hoped his would be, since the first reminded Wagner that he owed the Chief Accountant four kicks up the arse, the second that his secret vice was known to every girl in the office, and the third that every other Section Head was better paid than he was. And now for Christie's comprehensive masterstroke: he also put in a card attacking himself! Then he put in cards attacking Lucy and two other minor office celebrities, so that he would not himself stand out as the only one except Wagner to be the subject of attention!

These cards would be picked out and read, a fortnight after Christie had left the Section, by a Miss Drew whose main characteristic was that she was never able to keep anything to herself, including her what used to be known as ample charms.

It certainly made up, Christie thought, for the inconvenience of having to take his lunch an hour earlier.

One day on his way to work Christie read in his newspaper that the Home Secretary had dropped dead in the House during a late-night sitting. The cause was so far what the newspaper called a mystery.

As soon as sufficient noisy work was under way in the office for him to speak unnoticed, Christie picked up the telephone, dialled Scotland Yard and spoke as follows:

'Last night I got the Home Secretary. You do not know how I got him. Next I shall get the Minister for Trade and Industry, the Foreign Secretary, and the Prime Minister. In that order. You will not know how I got them, either.'

Then Christie put the phone down. He knew that even if the call were to be traced back to Tapper's the exact extension, amongst more than a hundred, could not be ascertained. Christie hoped that the call had been recorded other than by a constable's ear. Were all incoming phone calls to the police taped? Why not?

Headlam took Christie out for a drink at lunch time on his first day as a Wages Man, in celebration. They both drank bitter, this time.

'My father,' said Headlam, 'took me into a pub on my fifteenth birthday, stuck a pint of bitter into my hand and said: "Like all the men in this family, son, you do three things as a matter of course – you drink bitter, vote Labour, and support Chelsea." The bitter took some getting used to, as I'd been drinking brown up till then, but I was a Chelsea man already. As for Labour, I reckoned if you wanted to get on in the world you had to vote for the lot who had the money. But as I didn't have a vote then it didn't make much difference anyway.'

Headlam paused to provide a paragraph break for resting the reader's eye in what might otherwise have been a daunting mass of type.

'I was soon persuaded my father was right, however,' he went on, 'by an experience of some of those with the money. There was this girl who used to slum a bit down by the river, and she took something of a shine to me. And me to her, to be honest. She even introduced me to her family, who had one of those old houses along past the Doves. Sunday lunch, we had there. "D'you shoot pigeon, eh, what?" her father asks me, and "No," I reply, "But I do kick stones along the pavement at them sometimes." '

Christie was pleased to laugh.

'Didn't work out after that,' said Headlam, 'though she was a fair bit of grumble. Madge, her name was, Madge.'

Christie warmed and warmed to Headlam the more he came to know him. Indeed, such was the conjunction of sympathies that Christie was tempted to reveal his Great Idea to Headlam and enlist his help in carrying it towards its inevitable fruition. But his principles stayed him: *I am a cell of one!* In that way he could not be betrayed, in that way he was responsible for and to no one but himself. It was the only way; it had been proved to be the only way.

But in some ways Headlam was certainly a help to Christie's aims: unwittingly, of course, through providing those opportunities for Credits which the first Wages Round had revealed to him. And there were soon other ways in which Christie was helped by the kindly clerk who knew everybody and controlled (within strict limits, as I have said) some of the things they did or did not do. Headlam knew about the Tapper's Governors' private lift, for instance, for Headlam had once been (ante-

Lucy) sweet on the Company Secretary's secretary; and he was known and loved by everyone at Tapper's. Need I say more?

On his first Wages Round in his new Section Christie put one of his plans into practice. He had been able to carry out a further reconnaissance of the Boiler room on being asked by Headlam to go down and sort out a stoppages query from the same man Christie had seen on the first occasion. He had checked on the nature and position of the switches on the terminal boxes controlling (if he was to believe the Fore-boilerman) the whole of Tapper's power. And he had contrived a method of throwing these switches by remote control, so to speak, in an unusual way which I am not going to bother to invent on this occasion. But I will go so far as to tell you that it involved a shovel, which was naturally already there and available for use, a length of nylon twine, and a small, hard ball of compressed rubber of the kind delighted in by many children of all ages; and that once this apparatus had worked, then the only objects left were a shovel, which had every right to be there, and a child's ball with about a yard of twine attached. Furthermore, since the ball had been chosen for its remarkable, even improbable, bouncing capabilities, it would carry the twine a considerable distance away from the shovel when it fell; and might, indeed, if it lodged under one of the boilers or in some other inaccessible place, remain unfound for a considerable number of years, not to say until eventual (for it comes to all) demolition.

Christie set it on a Friday, payday; and since the timing of devices dependent on the strength of nylon twine has definite aleatoric limitations, he could not tell when it would plunge Tapper's into darkness and confusion. It might happen before he went home; more likely it would occur over the weekend at some time; or possibly it could still be primed early the next week.

When he came back to work on Monday it was no part of his duty to enquire as to whether there had been power failures that weekend; he was rigidly following his principles, of course. He knew there were certain continuous processes (DOOM DOOM and the Sugarboilers, for instance) which would be affected if it had occurred at the weekend; but that it would be better if it occurred during working hours of the working week.

There was no loss of power during that week; and on the Friday Wages Round Christie noticed as expected that his apparatus was no longer in place. Either it had worked during the weekend, or it had been discovered and dismantled at some other time. Or it had not worked. Christie never knew; this novel is not an unrelieved progression of successes, you know.

'What I would like to,' said Headlam, 'do is to make a discovery of the kind that a legendary employee of a well-known manufacturer of matches did.'

'What was that?' asked Christie.

'He went to his Governors and said he had an idea which would save them so many thousands a year. In return he wanted a salary for life of half those thousands. And their Governors were nothing like as dim as the Tapper's lot are. They agreed. And the man said "Put sandpaper on one side of the box instead of two." Which had never occurred to the Governors before. Perhaps they weren't much brighter than our lot, after all. But they were honourable, and half of what they saved on sandpaper they dutifully handed over for the rest of the man's natural life.'

'Haven't I heard that story before?' said Christie.

'I don't know,' said Headlam, crying into his beer, 'I don't know, how could I? But since I seem to be the comic relief in this novel . . .'

'It needs it,' said Christie.

'. . . have you heard about the man who asked a petshop owner if he had any dogs going cheap?'

'No,' said Christie, 'I don't think I have.'

'Ah,' said Headlam, 'In that case you won't have heard either that the petshop owner replied that he hadn't, his dogs went woof-woof!'

'I wish I still hadn't, now,' said Christie, and it was his turn to weep into his bitter.

It was at the end of his second week on Wages Section that Christie first became consciously curious about his income tax.

Each week they have deducted it, thought Christie, Tapper's, and now for two weeks I have abetted them in docking tax from others including Nutladies, Icers, and most of the rest. What are they doing? What am I doing?

And Christie understood that Tapper's held on to this money they deducted for as long as they legally could, and sometimes longer, and collected interest on it the while, or used it to lessen the interest they paid on their various overdrafts, and then paid it to the Collector of Taxes.

'Where does this Collector of Taxes have his office?' asked Christie of Headlam one morning.

'Brook Green Road,' said Headlam, 'just past the Palais.'

'Just past the Palais?' said Christie, 'Just past the Palais!'

'Yes,' said Headlam, 'just where it starts to curve towards the Bush.'

At once Christie began to try to imagine what this Collector of Taxes did with the money he garnered from, together with Tapper's numerous others, Christie. He no doubt passes it on to the Government, he thought, after keeping a modicum for his trouble. And he could at once think of innumerable things the Government spent it on of which he disapproved.

'The buggers!' said Christie, who I must point out yet again was very simple, 'And it's with my money, too! I shall allow no sufflamination in balancing that Debit!'

Luckily no one overheard him.

That very lunch hour he set out down Brook Green Road to where the Collector of Taxes had his office. Hythe House, he was astonished to see the building was named. Hythe, Christie knew, was a variant spelling of *hithe*, which meant a small port, haven, or landing-place, especially on a river: now only usually found as a place-name element, as in Rotherhithe, Lambeth (lamb-hithe), and so on. So this building, though relatively recent, must reflect in its name some landing-place on the Thames nearby: certainly not the pleasureboat stage above the Bridge, thought Christie, which is modern within my time, but another structure, older, hallowed by use from time immemorial and enshrined in the consciousness of a cultured Collector of Taxes. Ah. And Christie reflected that since *hithe* or *hythe* was not found in any other Teutonic (as they will say) language, this Collector of Taxes must indeed be a true patriot, no mere macaronic dabbler, he! I shall have to think of something really special for such a man, thought Christie, for this is a Collector who knows about far more than mere Debits and Credits, Fra Luca, filthy lucre, and so on!

Christie prowled around his mind that night, as so often. And of course it came to him, how he would acquit the Collector of Taxes.

It was easy. The Little Vermifuge, he named it, the train.

Next to Hythe House was a building site, the early stage of some extension necessary to contain the vaster amounts they planned to take from him and others, Christie imagined. The basic services were just being completed, amongst them, of course, the sewage pipes or (as they are more genteelly) the soil connections. They joined, economically, with those of the existing building, led off the ground floor executive cloakrooms which had been closed for the while and their exalted users provided with temporary (though no less comfortable) accommodation on the first floor. All this is necessary to understand, as you will shortly see, no doubt.

Next day Christie bought a clockwork train set. Already you can see what was in his mind. He was careful to handle nothing but the box. He had not heard about fingerprints in vain, oh no! Before making his duty (and pleasure) call on the Shrike that evening he carefully put on rubber gloves and to each of the five goods trucks of the train set he attached, by means of camera tape, a triad of gelignite sticks. Then he linked the wagons each to each in turn by detonator cord, coupled the whole to the engine and wound it up. An ordinary (but small) alarm clock completed Christie's evening's work before he packed it carefully away in a polyurethane-lined suitcase.

'Where,' you must be screaming, 'did Christie find his gelignite? I can't obtain gelignite. Not that I want to, of course.'

And that is your answer: if you want gelignite seriously enough, then you can come by it. ICI make it by the ton. Users use it by the hundredweight. Pounds of it are lost. Pounds are enough, for some people.

Christie wanted it more than enough.

The Shrike loved Christie. Then Christie loved the Shrike. Then they both loved each other, on the carpet in front of her gas fire.

Christie was not too late home; he liked to be in bed by twelve or so. At the site next to Hythe House he set the alarm to ring in twelve hours' time, released the catch which acted as a brake on the simple clockwork mechanism, and, perfectly, his little goods train ran its moderately-paced way up the clean nine-inch leadglazed pipe until it encountered a bend under Hythe House the radius of which was too small to permit its farther progress. So, after a clockwork squeal, it settled down to await the morrow. How touching.

Christie by then had reached the Palais, and was stopped by a police officer.

'What's in there?' said the police officer, indicating Christie's suitcase.

'Polyurethane chunks,' said Christie, honestly.

'Open it,' said the police officer, who was only a constable, other ranks, really.

'By what right . . .' began Christie.

'By every right,' said the constable. 'Open it!'

Christie did so.

The constable was disappointed, of course. Christie discussed with him the possibility of suing for wrongful suspicion, or something, but was advised that he would be better off scarpering before he got nicked for the next thing that came into the head of the constabulary.

I am told one has to put incidents like that in; for the suspense, you know.

Next day Christie and Headlam were amongst those who went to Hythe House at lunch time and gawped. They were also amongst the lucky ones: they saw three bodies brought out and were in one of the television news shots. How Christie bragged to the Shrike when they saw the news together that night! For he had been on television, and she had not! But she took it all in good part, of course, the lovely Shrike.

You begin to perceive a progression: Christie had begun in earnest!

CHAPTER XII

Scotland Yard is Baffled

'Someone,' said a slatternly Detective Inspector, 'is mucking us about.'

'Scotland Yard may be said to be baffled,' agreed the Assistant Chief Commissioner.

'It feels like the Anarchists again,' said the Chief Commissioner, one of whose ancestors had been by Winnie's shoulder at Sydney Street.

'The Anarchists!' said the other two, nearly in unison. And their jowls shook in silent laughter.

'If this gets any worse,' warned the Chief Commissioner, piqued, 'We shall have to consider the use of tactical nuclear weapons!'

CHAPTER XIII

Christie Argues with Himself!

I'm not trying to prove I'm right, but to find out whether.

Brecht

Later, Christie argued with himself. This was not common for him, as he was essentially one and in accord.

It was the first time he was aware that he had been more responsible than anyone else for a loss of human life.

Christie argued with himself. Who would win in the end? Should he have had this argument before the Little Vermifuge, and not after?

It went like this.

I have no right to kill people. No one has, according to all the arguments.

Yet people are killed. There are even licensed killers of people, of several kinds.

Despite the overwhelming concurrence with the canon regarding the absolute sanctity of human life, in fact society saw that human life was in fact a very inexpensive, plentiful and easily-disposable asset. Of all things, human life was the easiest to replace. A machine would be difficult, costly: but the man who drove or worked or manipulated it could be replaced at very short notice by any one of millions of other men, all equally capable after a little training, all equally replaceable.

Women were even cheaper.

Human life is cheap, dirt cheap, according to this society,

judged by the way it acts, the only true test, saw Christie, despite its pious mouthings. What it does in practice is not what it says it does. It does not care for human life: it shortens that life by the nature of the work it demands, it poisons that life in pursuit of mere profit, it organises wars from which it is certain mass killing will result . . . but you know the ways in which we are all diminished: I should not need to rehearse them further.

So Christie was easily able to become one again. If they fight dirty (and they do), so shall I, he thought; if they are so callous about human life, then so shall I be (though I could not possibly kill as many as they do).

Those who disagree are missing the point; it needs to be said, thought Christie. Of course the death of those near to one is distressing: of course the death of a mother makes one think she was indispensable. But if she really was indispensable, then you yourself die. Otherwise she was not indispensable. And in any case, society does not, they do not share any concern for your mother, what she meant to you. It could not be society if it did.

Christie could go on.

THE THIRD
RECKONING

. . . and many other things about which I will not extend myself too much here, because I have given you sufficient explanation above, and now you will be able to understand by yourself how to carry on, for accounts are nothing else but a due order of the fancy of a merchant, by which means he will have news of all his affairs, and he will easily know whether his business is going on well or not. As the proverb says: he who does business without knowing all about it sees his money turn into flies.

Pacioli

		DR AGGRAVATION					CR RECOMPENSE			
June	1	Balance brought forward	106	61	June	2	Torn poster		0	50
June	2	General diminution of Christie's life caused by advertising	50	00	June	2	Streetlamp glass		0	30
					June	2	Aldwych Theatre bomb hoax		3	81
June	8	Wagner's savage work- loads	7	00	June	5	Paper clips removed		0	01
June	8	Wagner's tonguelashing	3	50	June	6	Rubber stamp pad removed		0	02
June	9	General Wagner un- pleasantness	6	30	June	7	General removal of small items of stationery		0	06
June	30	General exploitation by Tapper's for month	200	00	June	13	Cabinet Minister call hoax		0	70
					June	21	Hythe House and the Little Vermifuge ∕		110	10
					June	30	Balance owing Christie carried forward to next Reckoning		257	91
			373	41					373	41

∕ Seven bodies, calculated at the
rate of 1.30 each being an allow-
ance for the commercial value of
the chemicals contained therein;
plus damage to property etc.

CHAPTER XIV

Christie sees the Possibilities as Endless

Shall I experiment with explosive mice, thought Christie? Or other small rodents? Bomb-carrying blackbirds? The possibilities were endless.

But Christie had to keep a sense of proportion, and remember his principles. A major attack should be followed by minor ones, or even no activity at all for a while, rather than another major one. Principle Six. Or was it Five?

For three days Christie restrained himself, abandoned himself at night to a closer and closer relationship with the Shrike, and during the day he allowed himself to be cultivated by Headlam.

On the fourth day he realised he might now continue at least the war of nerves, and so he used Tapper's telephone to inform the police that there was a bomb due in about ten minutes to make a mess of most of the London premises of Pork Pie Purveyors Ltd. This factory was opposite the window where Christie worked at his new job, and how he did enjoy seeing the workpeople spill tumultuously out of the gates! They were clearly delighted at having an excuse not to work, they laughed and chattered as they stood around at what they imagined to be a safe distance, in their bloody brown overalls and tidy caps, the men unusually with the women. Where the

PPP Governors were Christie could not see: he supposed them fled to the no doubt underground and private bunker they had prepared against the certainty of nuclear war.

After an hour's search the police declared that the phone call must have been a hoax, and went back to the station to eat the pork pies they had quietly pilfered.

There was little point in starting production afresh that day, so at lunchtime all the workpeople at PPP were sent home.

The possibilities were endless. While I live, Christie thought, and my life is virtually all before me, I do not need to think of my death.

Oh, the possibilities were endless!

CHAPTER XV

Christie (in his Wisdom) Overhears

Christie overheard a conversation amongst revolutionaries:

'We could attack the Clubs!'

'Yes!'

'Yes!'

'Yes!'

'They're good targets. Virtually unprotected. Full of people whose absence could well do some good.'

'We could start with the Alpine . . .'

'Then the American . . .'

'Then the American Women's . . .'

'Then the Anglo-Belgian . . .'

'Then the Army and Navy . . .'

'The Arts . . .'

'The Athenæum'

'The Authors' '

'The Bath'

'The Beefsteak'

'Boodle's'

'Brooks's'

'Buck's'

'The Caledonian'

'The Canning'
'The Carlton'
'The Cavalry'
'The Challoner'
'The Chemical'
'The City Livery'
A pause; then:
'One of us could get a job as bootboy in The Kennel.'
'Do they employ bootboys any more?'
'Yes. Bootboy in the Ladies' Alpine.'
'The Lansdowne'
'The London Fencing'
'The London Rowing'
'The MCC'
'The Mining'
'The Mining?'
'The Mining!'
Another pause.
'How about Pratt's?'
'A handful of sprats!'
'Be serious.'
'I am being serious.'
'Well, how about Pratt's?'
'Pratt's'
'The Public Schools'
'The Railway'
'Queen's'
'The Reform'
'The Roehampton'
'Just a minute. How do we decide which first?'
'Draw lots.'

'I know what that means, if you see what I mean, but what are lots?'

'How about The Savage?'

'The Savage'

'The Savile'

'The Service Women's'

'The Sesame Pioneer and Lyceum'

That one really stopped the revolutionaries. Christie waited. Then in time they began thinking aloud again.

'Socialism has never been given a chance in this country.'

'It must be given that chance.'

'We know what it's like to react against conservatism: now let's at least find out what it's like to react against socialism as the dominant idea.'

Another pause.

'After the Clubs we could defoliate Grosvenor Square.'

'Hyde Park!'

'Barnes Common!'

'Myddelton Square!'

Christie grimaced and passed out of overhearing; for these were but children.

CHAPTER XVI

Keep Britain Tidy; or,
Dispose of This Bottle Thoughtfully

Christie read how to fashion a Molotov Cocktail or petrol bomb.

Only very simple and easily-obtainable things were needed: that was the beauty of it.

A container; a screw of rag; some petrol; and a little paraffin.

The container had to shatter on impact, so glass or some kind of ceramic was most appropriate. Glass bottles are obtainable in their millions, and are therefore a natural favourite with the cocktail set. A milk bottle comes to mind first: but the milk bottle is generally a thick kind of a bottle, heavy. Everyone will have had experience of dropped milk bottles bouncing unharmed. The bottle must shatter easily for the purposes of the disaffected. No, by far the best bottle on the market for them has been provided by the soft drinks companies: half an imperial pint capacity, a screw cap of light gauge metal, glass walls of the very minimum thickness, a circumference so snug to the hand as to make accurate throwing relatively easy, and, being non-returnable, of such ready availability as to provoke ironic comment that the forces of conservatism are unwittingly providing the very instruments of their own discomfort.

As to the method. First of all one washed out the bottle of its (tonic, bitter lemon or whatever) dregs and allowed it to dry, neck downwards. While it was drying, one used a glasscutter to score the thin walls with at least four vertical strokes (this to make as near certain as may be that the bottle will indeed shatter on impact). Two cuts were then made with a sharp pointed knife in the cap, cruciform, and the four cruel points thus created deflected downwards to open a guarded hole. Through this hole one dragged the screw of rag, which was sufficiently bulky to be spiked by the four barbs; these could be pressed back, if necessary, to grip the rag securely. The bottle one then filled with petrol, the rag one soaked with paraffin and one then screwed the cap firmly on.

The Molotov Cocktail was now ready for throwing, requiring only that the projecting end of the rag be lit.

If it was thought desirable to undertake the preparation of a batch of bombs in advance, it was necessary only that the filling with petrol and the soaking with paraffin be left until just before the bombs were required to be used. Milk crates make reasonable bulk containers; less satisfactory are the cardboard cases in which the original soft drinks bottles came. A team of three may conveniently be employed to perform the following drill: one fills the bottles with petrol; the second dips the rags into paraffin and screws on the caps; and the third lights and throws.

What you throw them at is your own business, of course, thought Christie; but let no one be ungraith.

CHAPTER XVII

The No Doubt Welcome Return of the Shrike

'I don't know why I love you so much,' said the Shrike, stirring her tea, duchess-like, with the other hand, it being that week in the month, 'But I do, mystery man. And I don't ask any questions, just bring you home the odd pound of stuffed breast of lamb. . . .'

'What about some fillet steak, then?' said Christie, to take his mind somewhat farther off and thus prolong the delicious progress.

'You don't find fillet steak in a butcher's around here,' replied the Shrike, 'I'm sorry to say. It all goes to the restaurants, Mr Cameron says, or the West End butchers.'

'You're learning a lot,' said Christie.

And the delightful Shrike redoubled her efforts to please him, blowing on the purple tip now she was not required to converse, stroking and constricting and pulling as she had learnt to do as a child on a farm, handmilking.

The end came all too quickly, as it does at that age, and the Shrike watched ever entranced as the foamy pulses welled, calmed and died. That was understood to be coming.

Meanwhile, they were both perfectly happy. Well, this is fiction, is it not? Isn't it?

'I'm glad you don't work at Tapper's,' said Christie, 'I don't know how Headlam can keep his hands off Lucy all day.'

'Because he has them on her all night,' said the Shrike, who was quite a wit.

Christie loved the Shrike's room, as well. One wall was of matchboarding. Nothing could be heard through it. Another wall was of brick, faced with plaster and wallpaper. Yet another had a window in it. The penultimate had the door in it. The fifth wall was unusual in itself but otherwise unremarkable. The Shrike kept a photograph of Christie as a schoolboy hung up on it, to remind her. Out on the landing was the kitchen and the lavatory, though not necessarily in that order. The Shrike had decorated her room exquisitely, up stepladders with emulsion paint until all hours when she realised she was about to meet Christie. And she kept it beautifully, too. There was always a lucifer for Christie to light his cheroots, even though he never smoked. The ceiling was matchboarded, too, while the floorboards were painted and woodgrained to produce a striking *trompe l'oeil* effect. The Shrike was not by nature a butcher's assistant, Christie realised only too well: it was society that forced her to be so, or to be always something similar. She was as a pearl in her own right, and it was a reflection on society that it could find only inappropriate use for that wit, that nacreous quality that were just two of the things that endeared her to him.

'Enough of that metaphorical rubbish,' said the Shrike, 'What's wrong with stuffed breasts of lamb?'

'Nothing, in themselves,' said Christie, 'really. In fact I quite like them, as a change. But I feel what we eat is being dictated too much by Mr Cameron's meaty misjudgments on any given day.'

'I'll see what I can do,' said the goodhearted Shrike, 'but how can we be said to be perfectly happy a few lines back, and now be complaining about the monotony of the diet?'

'Easily,' smiled Christie.

The Shrike had a tea-set given to her by her grandmother. It pleased her very much, though not enough for her to be proud of it. That was far from her way of thinking, yes. Tea she poured from it, though.

'You could go and work for Pork Pie Purveyors Ltd,' said Christie, 'now they've been invented. That would be a logical progression of the kind that very much appeals to the vast majority of readers.'

'Not me,' said the Shrike, emphatically, 'someone's got it in for them. Didn't you hear the other day they had a bomb threat?'

CHAPTER XVIII

Christie's Biggest Yet

Christie in a fine pub.

I have broken a Principle, thought Christie, number Eleven if I remember correctly. Only now do I think of it. I not only watched but enjoyed the exodus of employees from PPP. If I am not careful, I shall be caught.

Christie liked a drink. He put it down to the mixed blood in him. All the races liked a drink, mixed drinks for preference. Anything could be explained if your blood was mixed, and whose was not?

Again drinking Guinness, Christie lodged himself at the bar where he could listen to a green man who looked as though he might well provide him with the key to his biggest Credit yet.

'I got it all off,' said the green man demotically to his large companion, 'I'll scrub the floor for her, buy her strawberries and suchlike to placate her, then if she still keeps on I tell her she'll never stop me fishing. I'm not out after other women, or lifting me elbow more than once a week, but I'll go on fishing till I turns me toes up.'

'Where do you do most of your fishing?' asked the large man, politely.

'Mostly over the reservoirs at Barn Elms,' said the green man, 'just the other side of the bridge there. It's not bad, though it's nothing like what it was in the war and just after. I came home from North Africa in 1943 bomb-happy, and to help me in my convalescence my doctor and me persuaded the Metropolitan Water Board to let me go fishing over Barn Elms. All reservoirs were forbidden ground during the war, see, restricted, restricted areas, for obvious reasons. And of course since no one had been fishing, the water was stiff with fish. I had the time of my life! I took a pike from there one evening that weighed nineteen and threequarter pounds, nineteen and threequarter pounds! What a doctor's tonic that was! Took me an hour and a quarter to land him. I sold it down Hammersmith Market next morning for thirty bob, and when the fishmonger cut it open what d'you think there was inside?'

'A whole duck,' said the large man.

'That's right – a whole duck,' said the green man. 'You must have heard the story before, you sod.'

Christie had heard it before, too, like many stories; but he had not until now been able to place this one in a Double-Entry context. Now he could!

It is well known that people are careless in their disposal of cyanide waste, people in the plating and metal-finishing industries in particular, that is. So you do not need me to explain how Christie came by enough for his Book-keeping purposes. But since you will know (or can easily check) that the reservoirs in question cover several acres and are filled to a depth of between fifteen and twenty feet depending on the season, you will want to know how Christie transported and transferred the large quantity implied by the results achieved. But do you know what dilute quantities of cyanide are respectively safe, sickening, and fatal?

Christie simply found a plating works by reference to his telephone directory, and from his library ascertained what cyanide looked like, in what it was kept and how it was handled, and then one evening about eight he went there and gained entrance to the yard through the small door in the gate by means of his plastic bank card fiddled through between the Yale-type lock striker and its striking plate. The commonest method known to criminal man; I am almost ashamed to repeat it.

The lorry was already loaded with drums of the chemical, as Christie knew from his lunchtime reconnaissance it would be. He loosened the caps with a chain wrench, and removed them with heavy-duty rubber gloves on. Starting the lorry by bridging across the ignition switch took a little more time than opening the door, but was equally as simple and does not bear further elucidation here. Then he opened the gates, drove out, closed the gates, drove on across Hammersmith Bridge and turned fourth left into Merthyr Terrace, no martyr. No one was of course on duty at this time of night to see him cut the u-bolt of the padlock with one brachyureate nip of a pair of boltcutters, open the gates and drive in.

Christie did not waste time looking. A short track led up the bank of the reservoirs, and at the nearest point he reversed the lorry to the edge and actuated the tip-up mechanism the lorry (of course) had. As the drums began to rumble through the open tailgate, Christie jumped out and watched them. In the low sunlight he saw the crystalline white powder pour out, begin to dissolve and make its way into the planet's water.

'I was not breaking Principle Eleven again,' Christie told me later, 'since this was a cause, not an effect.'

How could I disagree with him?

So he sent the tip-up down again, and drove off. He knew that he could not drive off while the tip-up was coming down, and thus save time, because tip-up lorries do not work like that: while the engine is driving the tip-up mechanism through the gearbox, it cannot drive the roadwheels too. It could, it is technically possible; but that is not the way gearboxes are in general designed.

And Christie returned the lorry whence it came, happy in his evening's work. It seems always he returns to the bosom of the Shrike: but wouldn't you?

ICI make all the cyanide in this country; but that is the second credit they have received in this novel.

Radio and television were broadcasting warnings by shortly after ten o'clock the next morning. Many people heard them. Most of the dead were in west London. They had taken it with breakfast, as tea, coffee, reconstituted fruit juice, or squash. A number had drunk straight from the tap, as it came. In old houses, some had (little good it did them) let the tap run for two minutes to run off water standing overnight and therefore having a high lead content imparted by the pipes.

Not a pretty sight, eh? Think what it would have been like if it had been cadmium (twenty-five times more toxic than cyanide) or chromates (fifty times more toxic) or beryllium (two thousand five hundred times!). You may consider it fortunate that Christie did not know about beryllium at the time.

The Shrike drank nothing but milk in the mornings, for her complexion. So did Headlam and Lucy, perhaps the only other sympathetic characters in this novel so far; apart from Christie's mother, whom cyanide could not materially affect.

A total of just over twenty thousand people died of cyanide poisoning that morning. This was the first figure that came to hand as it is roughly the number of words of which the novel consists so far.

Be assured there are not many more, neither deaths nor words.

Their deaths were not painful, nor prolonged. Virtually all of them (as I have explained before: but it is important) were easily replaceable, according to society. What can be wrong? Can Christie be condemned?

Christie himself wondered: am I not overdrawn? What wrong has society done me that I can offset more than twenty thousand deaths against it?   Everything, he decided after a pause, everything.

The wrongs done to fifty-odd million others, for just a start.

But what about their relatives, you must be asking. What about their relatives? They will blame it on the Government, argued Christie, and not on me. And that is entirely proper: the Government is responsible in every way for letting such things be and become and remain possible. Guilt at a Double-Entry overdraft or personal responsibility would be liberal wishiwashiness. One must subtly oppose the Government with its own weapons of casualness, indifference, mass carelessness.

Three days later, having read in the evening papers what the Government maintained were definitive totals of the dead, and succoured the Shrike, Christie left her in a deep post-coital sleep and returned home to catch up on his accounts.

THE FOURTH
RECKONING

. . . otherwise, not being a good accountant in your affairs, you will
have to feel your way forward like a blind person, and much loss
can arise therefrom; therefore with deep study and care make efforts
above all to be a good accountant. The manner in which to become
one with ease I have fully and sufficiently described to you in this
sublime work, with all its rules duly given in their correct places
so that you will be able to find everything in the present treatise
which without doubt will be very useful to you; and remember to
pray to God for me that, to His praise and glory, I may proceed by
working from good to better.

Pacioli

	DR AGGRAVATION				CR RECOMPENSE			
July 1	Balance brought forward	257	91	July 5	Pork Pie Purveyors Ltd. bomb hoax		2	40
July 7	Socialism not given a chance	311,398	00	July 10	Ready availability of non-returnable bottles		0	07
July 9	The Shrike not given a chance commensurate with her abilities	40,734	62	July 27	Death of 20,479 innocent west Londoners ⨍		26,622	70
				July 31	Balance owing to Christie carried forward to next Reckoning		325,765	36
		352,390	53				352,390	53
					⨍ Calculated at the same rate (1.30 per head) as in Third Reckoning; negligible damage to property involved, you will be relieved to hear.			

CHAPTER XIX

The Shrike's Old Mum; a Use for Shaving
Foam scarcely Envisaged by the
Manufacturers; and the Shrike's Last Rule

The Shrike's Old Mum lived, as you already know, up in Islington. Islington is certainly up from Hammersmith, which is only some sixteen feet above sea level, whereas old Islington lies mainly on a ridge whose southernmost point is Claremont Square in Finsbury. The exact height of Claremont Square escapes me for the moment, though I could look it up. Yes, I will.   It is just above the hundred foot contour line, say fifteen feet, making a height of a hundred and fifteen feet in all. Claremont Square must have been a fine point to view the City and the river at one time, before it was built on. But of course that is not really relevant for our purposes, since the Shrike's Old Mum lived just on the eastern side of the ridge, down off Essex Road, at the flats in Britannia Row. And I am not going out with theodolite and mate to determine just where she lived in relation to the hundred foot contour line, or to work out how high her flat took her above it in relation to ground level; no, not for you: nor anyone.

'Come and see my Old Mum,' the Shrike had said, and Christie had been pleased.

'How are you, Old Mum?' he said warmly and politely when they had gained entrance to her flat.

'I was bombed out in the war,' said the Shrike's Old Mum, 'it sears you, an experience like that, you know.'

Christie knew.

'Lost me Old Man, too,' she went on, 'leastways, they never found him. Sitting just across from the fire he was at the time. Nothing left. Not a sign. Could I have fallen asleep and he'd gone out to water the dog? Of course not. That cow Stegginson spread that about. . . .'

Christie started at the coincidence.

'. . . but the cow'll live to regret it! Brought her up on me own, I did, me daughter, isn't she a fine girl? I'll bet you don't half enjoy her, don't you, young man?'

Christie nodded, unembarrassed, pleased at this rapport with the Old Mum.

'Aaaaer, it was worth it, all those years of sacrifice, just to get my daughter placed in a respectable novel like this, you know. It's my crowning achievement. And with only one leg, too!'

The Shrike's Old Mum suddenly took off an artificial limb which had hitherto been unapparent to Christie, and waved it triumphantly.

'Stick of bombs, it was,' went on the Shrike's Old Mum, 'the first got St Mary's Church in Upper Street, the second got that brothel on the corner of Dagmar Terrace, and the third got me and my Old Man.'

'The church, sex, and marriage,' observed Christie, laughing, 'that's too neat.'

'That's how it happened,' said the Shrike's Old Mum, 'you can't muck about with how it happened, can you?'

'I'll have a word with you later about your obsession with knocking religion,' said the Shrike to Christie, quietly and without venom, 'And we must go now, Old Mum, Sunday's the only day we have for a really long fuck. Cheerio. Ring if you want us for anything. See you Tuesday night as usual.'

'And who said we were married anyway?' shouted the Shrike's Old Mum after them, slowly lifting the leg to wave them goodbye.

Later that Sunday Christie and the Shrike really concentrated on it. The Shrike's present delight was to be covered in shaving foam (applied by Christie with an aerosol) from neck to ankles, paying particular attention to the erogenic zones, of course. Christie then used a safety razor to shave off the foam, slowly, paying even more attention to the erogenic zones, and thus providing the Shrike with a small series of minor orgasms (she was lucky that way) before Christie gave her a big one by a good going over (or into, rather) with his subtly-nicknamed Jonathan Thomas.

Oh, and by the way: the safety razor had no blade in it.

An expensive way to use aerosol shaving foam, of course, but it was Sunday.

Then they had a bath together, and afterwards the Shrike removed all further traces of the shaving foam with a well-known brand of carpet shampoo. From the carpet, that is. It was the last of her three rules.

Christie was preparing the supper when the Shrike uttered the word she had promised earlier in relation to Christie's abuse of religion:

'Why?'

'Because it's there,' explained Christie, patiently, to his beloved, 'as long as it's there and has so much power then it must be open to attack. It's been continuously discredited throughout its history, but it's still there and it still goes on with its confidence tricks as though nothing much had happened. It's corrupt, lying, inefficient, useless, and rapacious. To name but a few. What d'you expect me to do – love it?'

'But what can you do about it, darling?' said the Shrike.

'Ah,' said Christie, and thought to himself: what can I do about it?

CHAPTER XX

Not the Longest Chapter in this Novel

A great lorry belched its long bulk into Tapper's delivery bay.

'Sign here,' said the driver, 'Your order number 325,765/36. Five tons of carbon paper.'

CHAPTER XXI

In which Christie and I have it All Out; and which You may care to Miss Out

. . . the novel, during its metamorphosis in respect of content and form, necessarily regards itself ironically. It denies itself in parodistic forms in order to be able to outgrow itself.

Széll Zsuzsa
Válságés regény (p. 101)
Akadémia (Hungary) 1970
transl. by Novák Gyorgy

'Christie,' I warned him, 'it does not seem to me possible to take this novel much further. I'm sorry.'

'Don't be sorry,' said Christie, in a kindly manner, 'don't be sorry. We don't equate length with importance, do we? And who wants long novels anyway? Why spend all your spare time for a month reading a thousand-page novel when you can have a comparable aesthetic experience in the theatre or cinema in only one evening? The writing of a long novel is in itself an anachronistic act: it was relevant only to a society and a set of social conditions which no longer exist.'

'I'm glad you understand so readily,' I said, relieved.

'The novel should now try simply to be Funny, Brutalist, and Short,' Christie epigrammatised.

'I could hardly have expressed it better myself,' I said, pleased, 'I've put down all I have to say, or rather I will have done in another twenty-two pages, so surely. . . .'

'So I do go on a little longer?' interrupted Christie.

'Yes, Christie, you go on to the end,' I assured him, and myself went on: 'Surely no reader will wish me to invent anything further, surely he or she can extrapolate only too easily from what has gone before?'

'If there is a reader,' said Christie. 'Most people won't read it.'

'Politicians, policemen, some educators and many others treat "most people" as idiots.'

'So writers may too?'

'On the contrary. "Most people" are right not to read novels today.'

'You've said all this before.'

'I'm very likely to say it again, too, since it's true.'

A pause. Then suddenly Christie said:

'Your work has been a continuous dialogue with form?'

'If you like,' I replied diffidently.

'Only one of the things it's been,' said Christie generously. 'It's something to aspire to, becoming a critic! Though there are too many exclamation marks in this novel already.'

Another pause. One of the girls in what is ill-reputed to be a brothel opposite hung out the shirt of what might be her ponce. Christie smiled gently, turned back to me.

'But I am to go on for a while?'

'Of course,' I assured him again.

'Until I have everything?'

'Yes, Christie, until you have everything.'

CHAPTER XXII

In which an Important Question is
Answered; and Christie thinks he has
Everything

Christie had lunch in the Stromboli Café in the Broadway, on his own, without Headlam or anyone else he knew. The place was not very pretentious, but the food was made tasty and it was cheap.

Today, however, there was a beetle in Christie's portion of beef curry, rice, and chips. It was a black beetle, though whether it was a blackbeetle or cockroach (which is not properly a beetle at all, not coleopterous but orthopterous) Christie was not at this time concerned to establish. Heaving with disgust, as they say, he denied himself further curry, let alone a sweet, paid, and went out to buy himself a whisky which he drank in one small draught in the hope that it would kill anything unpleasant in the way of viri, germs, or bacilli which he might have just ingested.

As soon as he was once more at his desk in Tapper's Wages Section Christie reached out for the telephone directories. He found the number of the local government offices, rang, and asked for the Health Department. When they answered he rapidly suggested a check on the Stromboli Café kitchens where he was sure they would find evidence to justify a prosecution. Then he rang off without revealing his identity.

When he reached home, tired, that evening Christie

wondered whether he had time or energy for these small Credits. Then he remembered Principle Six (was it?) again and travelled to a public telephone at Willesden to make a call to the police suggesting that in the Stromboli Café during its most patronised period, now, there were several pounds of gelignite set to go off in twenty minutes.

'Or possibly ten, if I've made a mistake,' he added, casually, and let the handpiece fall from his gloved hand.

But Christie was certainly aware that he had bigger things to do. It was all very well expressing himself and balancing things up by the death of twenty thousand-odd people, he thought, but now greater things are expected of me, by me. A Natural Progression must be maintained. This time I shall go not for numbers but for quality, very loosely speaking. The greatest number of those who make most of the decisions affecting me gathered together at any one time is probably at the State Opening of Parliament. To obliterate the buildings concerned at that time would rid us at one blow of the Monarch and other assorted members of the Royal Household, The Cabinet, The Opposition Leaders and all other MPs who were not sick, malingering, or lucky.

Yes!

Christie first considered that a limited tactical nuclear weapon of a type similar to that referred to on page 111 would be most suitable for this purpose: he would acquire one from the appropriate military establishment, hire a light aircraft and drop it at the height of the proceedings. But then he remembered Principle Five, and realised that this method was beyond his means, involved a very high risk of being caught, and was unnecessary anyway. All that was needed were orthodox explosive charges set at the south-west and south-east base corners of Big Ben and large enough to bring the whole thing down on to the Chamber of the House of Commons. It might not rid us of quite as many of the quality, but that was unavoidable; and those surviving would certainly be greatly terrified, thought Christie. And for the first time I shall employ one of the products of modern electronic wizardry: a radio-controlled time fuse effective up to a radius of two miles. I shall take that morning off work, and I shall proceed to a pub in Charing Cross Road for a Guinness. At about ten past eleven, having given the Monarch and Parliament time to settle down, I shall convey to them my little electronic message.

Guy Fawkes and I together, Christie thought, with the difference that he was caught.

The question should be asked: what did the Shrike see in Christie?

And be answered: everything.

'I do not know what your mission in life is,' said the Shrike, 'but I do know that I shall do all I can to help you to achieve it!'

'Darling,' said Christie, 'give us a kiss.'

Now, thought Christie, I have everything.

CHAPTER XXIII

Now Christie really does have Everything

Within five days the Shrike had given up her flat and moved into Christie's house. It was just as though she had always been there: now I can really achieve something in life, thought Christie.

And during that same five days he had consulted a quarto work in the AA library which reproduced Barry's original drawings detailing the construction of the base of Big Ben; undertaken a reconnaissance which had shown him that security arrangements were (as all are) not insuperable, and, furthermore, that two additional but larger charges placed at the north-west and north-east corners of the Victoria Tower would bring that down on the House of Lords, just in case they happened to be there; ascertained and acquired the exact quantity of gelignite necessary for the purpose; and purchased very reasonably the simple electronic equipment which would send a short-wave signal to his parcels: one peep for Big Ben, two for the Victoria Tower.

On Tuesday, the sixth day, however, Christie, soldered to the Shrike with need and common love, was woken up by the touch of her hands feeling in an exploratory rather than an erotic way.

'You have a lump there,' said the Shrike.

175

'What d'you expect if you're so irresistible?' said Christie.

'Not there, there,' said the Shrike, indicating a place just under Christie's ribcage on the right side.

Christie felt.

'Yes,' he said, 'I have a lump.'

He felt himself abdominally as a whole. Paused. Then said: 'In fact, I seem to have an attack of the lumps!'

The Shrike began keening.

'I have had a certain unwonted lassitude recently. For instance, a certain job has just taken me five days to prepare when normally I would have completed it in three. And now I have this attack of the lumps,' Christie told the doctor, jokily.

'Riddled with it.'

The surgeon saw no reason to use anything but cliché in reporting to the Shrike on the exploratory operation.

The Shrike cried herself blind.

'Now I really do have everything,' said Christie as the Shrike and her Old Mum came to the hospital bedside, 'including cancer.'

'I shall never be able to look at an aerosol can of shaving foam again,' said the Shrike, putting a brave face on it.

'I shan't need one either,' said Christie, 'this radiotherapy kills the roots of the bristles and renders shaving unnecessary.'

The Shrike's Old Mum took out her silver-mounted tear bottle.

'But it was good, wasn't it,' Christie went on, 'the last one, all of them?'

'There'll be more,' hoped the Shrike against hope.

The surgeon had never seen it spread so far, develop so rapidly. Such people have an infinite capacity for surprise.

Defenceless under the cobalt gun, through the terror Christie's mind still worked:

. . . I need not have bothered, need I, it seems, if it all ends like this: but if not like this for others it still ends. A mockery of *hope, of thinking of the next day. So I need not have bothered: all is useless, pointless, waste*

all, all pointless

'At least your Great Idea prevented you from becoming bored to death with life,' I told Christie when I paid what he must have seen as my last visit to him.

'Of no concern now,' replied Christie, weakly, 'But what does concern me is that they'll never know whether the charges were primed, or even planted, or if they went off by accident, or anything.'

'That's life,' was the only thing I could think of to say.

'Life goes on,' riposted Christie, smiling at how we had both relapsed into cliché, as usually happens at moments of extreme emotion. 'Just like in Shakespeare: bring on Fortinbras and cart off the corpses.'

He paused. I thought it was his exhausted condition, but he was considering something deeply.

'Shakespeare has been overtaken now,' he said eventually, 'by events. Life might very well not go on, for either or both of the reasons.'

I had to agree. There was not even that consolation any longer. Christie appeared weaker, closing his eyes and breathing through his mouth rather than his nose. Then he suddenly rallied:

'Amongst those left are you,' he said, accusingly.

'So far,' I said.

'Will the Shrike go on?' he asked.

'I don't know. I've grown very fond of her. Perhaps another time,' I answered, as honestly as I could.

'I hope she does go on,' said Christie.

A pause.

'And I'm very fond of you, too, by now, Christie,' I told him. But he gave no sign of having heard, had moved on one stage nearer.

Ten minutes, and again he was suddenly lucid:

'Soon,' he said, his old bright self in speech at least, 'they'll discover a cure for cancer. And that will make you look stupid. You'll be knackered! The cause may be so obvious, then. Like nineteenth-century surgeons used to operate with aprons caked with the blood and pus of earlier operations. The thicker it was, the more esteemed the surgeon. They didn't understand then about germs and cross-infection. They seem stupid to us now, and you'll seem stupid when they find out about cancer! Just think, it may have been caused through those misshapes I had on page 67!'

Christie's eyes remained open, bright. But I cannot say he looked flushed.

'In any case,' he said, almost to himself, not looking at me, 'you shouldn't be bloody writing novels about it, you should be out there bloody doing something about it.'

And the nurses then suggested I leave, not knowing who I was, that he could not die without me.

CHAPTER XXIV

The Actual End, leading to . . .

In the image of yourself, Christie is, remember.

His average eyes appeared sunken, ringed with yellow-brown; his average cheeks had sunk, too. The general feeling about Christie now is one of sinking.

Not without trace.

So that the whole face seemed like a caricature of its earlier self, the mouth assumed an unnatural rictus, the skin became tauter and greyer, the lines standing out more whitely.

Now at shorter and shorter intervals he made them aware of his need for the cushioning drugs. They gave them to him, palliatives, morphine derivatives, then heroin itself.

When pneumonia set in the other patients quickly noticed and called it the death rattle. In deference to them they moved Christie into a side ward on his own. They did not treat the pneumonia: there was no point, though strictly they should have done.

Christie they kept unconscious.

Xtie died.

... THE FINAL RECKONING